BEW~~...~~
DO NOT ~~....~~
BOOK FROM BEGINNING TO END!

You can't believe it! You stare out of the window at the creepy cemetery behind your grandmother's back garden. The graves are moving! You're sure of it. Then you turn to see an even more frightening sight—your grandmother's house is haunted by ghosts. Lots of ghosts. Evil ghosts who want you!

Why are the creeping coffins creeping? Do you stay to find out or do you race home—where there's a terrifying ghost waiting for you?

If you stay you discover that the coffins are spelling a message in the graveyard—a message that spells out your doom. Unless you can find the ghost who is the Keeper of the Sword, steal the sword and plunge it into the grave of the MPG! What's an MPG? You'll have to find out for yourself—but hurry, the ghosts are moving closer and closer . . .

You're in control of this scary adventure. You decide what will happen. And how terrifying the scares will be!

Start on page 1. Then follow the instructions at the bottom of each page. You make the choices.

SO TAKE A DEEP BREATH. CROSS YOUR FINGERS. AND TURN TO PAGE 1 NOW TO *GIVE YOURSELF GOOSEBUMPS!*

READER BEWARE—
YOU CHOOSE THE SCARE!

Look for more
GIVE YOURSELF GOOSEBUMPS adventures
from R. L. STINE:

1 *Escape From the Carnival of Horrors*
2 *Tick Tock, You're Dead!*
3 *Trapped in Bat Wing Hall*
4 *The Deadly Experiments of Dr Eeek*
5 *Night in Werewolf Woods*
6 *Beware of the Purple Peanut Butter*
7 *Under the Magician's Spell*

Give Yourself Goosebumps

The Curse of the
Creeping Coffin

R. L. Stine

Scholastic Children's Books
Commonwealth House, 1–19 New Oxford Street, London WC1A 1NU, UK
a division of Scholastic Ltd
London ~ New York ~ Toronto ~ Sydney ~ Auckland

First published in the USA by Scholastic Inc., 1996
First published in the UK by Scholastic Ltd, 1998

Copyright © Parachute Press, Inc., 1996
GOOSEBUMPS is a trademark of Parachute Press, Inc.

ISBN 0 590 11247 3

Typeset by Rowland Phototypesetting Ltd, Bury St Edmunds, Suffolk
Printed by Cox & Wyman Ltd, Reading, Berks.

10 9 8 7 6 5 4 3 2 1

"I'm bored," you moan. "I'm so bored, I could eat flies. Just to see how they taste."

"Flies have germs," your grandmother replies.

It is a hot, sticky day in the middle of July. You plop down into a creaky old chair in your grandmother's kitchen. Your parents dropped you off yesterday, before they left for their holiday. And already you could die of boredom.

Your grandmother's old dog, Sparkle, yawns loudly. He crawls under the table. Moments later, he begins to snore.

"I know just how you feel, Sparkle," you say. You sigh loudly.

"Why don't you go outside and find something to do?" your grandmother suggests. She looks up from the pie she's baking and nods towards the back garden.

Go out there? you think. Into her back garden? No way.

You glance out of the window. It's probably ninety degrees in the shade, but you shiver. Your grandmother's house is right in front of an old cemetery. Rows and rows of old, crumbling tombstones sit just beyond the edge of her back garden.

But that's not what scares you.

What scares you is that the tombstones have been moving!

Go on to PAGE 2.

2

You noticed it right after you arrived yesterday.

You saw the tombstones from your bedroom window on the first floor. You could tell some of the graves had cool carvings on them, so you decided to go outside and take a closer look.

But when you entered the graveyard, something was different. Strange.

Some of the graves were out of place.

Nah, can't be, you told yourself. Graves don't disappear.

But still . . .

From your bedroom window, you could have sworn there were six or seven graves in the back row.

Now there were only three!

Nah . . . You must have counted wrong. You decided to forget it and went to bed.

But when you woke up this morning and glanced out of the window, the coffins had moved again.

Now there were *ten* in the back row! And the middle rows seemed more crowded. It almost looked as if some of the graves were moving forwards and some of the graves were moving backwards, and there was a big traffic jam in the centre.

The coffins were rearranging themselves!

But how? And why?

Go on to PAGE 3.

Your grandmother taps you on the shoulder. She snaps you out of your day-dream. "Go on," she says. "Go and play outside."

Outside? Out *there*? You shudder as you glance out of the kitchen window again. "Oh, no," you cry. "It's disappeared!"

"What's disappeared?" your grandmother asks.

"The grave with the angel on it!" you screech, pointing out of the window. "It's gone!"

One headstone in particular caught your eye yesterday. It had an angel carving on it. The angel looked so realistic you practically believed she could fly away.

Did she?

Your grandmother peers out of the kitchen window. "Don't be a goose," she scolds you. "That tombstone is still there."

You don't answer her. You can't. Your heart is pounding crazily and your mouth has gone dry. You bolt out of the back door. You've got to see for yourself.

But in the graveyard you discover that your grandmother is right. The tombstone with the angel hasn't gone.

It's just moved!

It had been in the last row. Now it's up the front.

I'm losing my mind, you think. Losing it completely.

Or are you?

Find out on PAGE 4.

You run back into the house shouting.

"Grandma!" you yell. "That grave with the angel on it—"

Your grandmother interrupts you. "You don't have to shout, dear. The angel?" She looks up from her pie crust. "That's a nice one. Let me see. Who was buried there? Oh, yes. That's Elmyra Martin's grave."

Before you can explain about the moving gravestones, a voice on the far side of the room makes you jump. "The name is *Elvira* Martin," the voice says sharply. "Not Elmyra. You never *could* get my name right!"

Your mouth drops open. A strange woman now stands in the doorway that leads from the kitchen into the hall.

A very strange woman. Because she isn't a living, breathing woman. She's a ghost!

"Uh, Grandma . . . ?" you begin. But from the way your granny is humming to herself, you can tell she doesn't hear or see this scary visitor.

"And don't *you* stare at me, you little wretch," the ghost says, pointing at you. "Or you'll be sorry."

What are you going to do? Suddenly you're living in a haunted house!

If you run outside, turn to PAGE 18.
If you talk to the ghost, turn to PAGE 25.

To your amazement, it works! The horse grows smaller.

Hey—cool!

You push the volume button down again. Like magic, the ghost-horse grows even smaller.

"Wow!" you shout. You start pushing other buttons on the TV remote control. You can hardly wait to see what will happen!

Unbelievably, when you press the CHANNEL button—the one that moves up to the next channel—the ghost-horse changes into something else! A ghostly kung-fu master!

When you press the button again, the kung-fu ghost changes into the ghost of an Egyptian pharaoh.

"This is amazing!" you exclaim.

Then you press it one more time.

Uh-oh. Big mistake.

Turn to PAGE 129.

You turn and run from Lark. But he's gaining on you. And his friends have joined in the chase.

"Let's get those little creeps!" Lark's friends are shouting.

You and Robin are skidding round a corner when you hear a voice whisper in your ear. "I'll help you—on one condition. You have to promise to do whatever I ask tomorrow."

It's the ghost-boy! You can't see him, but you heard his offer. What are you going to do?

If you accept the ghost's offer, turn to PAGE 52.

If not, turn to PAGE 59.

Yuck! Everything in the bucket spills all over your hair, head, face, shoulders and shirt.

Raw eggs. Warm Coke. Sour milk. Bread crumbs. It's disgusting.

Some used tissues are mixed in there, too.

"What did you do that for?" you yell angrily.

"You saw the sign," Digger replies. "No trespassers. That means *you*."

What a creep! you think. Digger is a total, certified jerk.

In other words, he's just what you need to deal with this ghost!

So what are you going to do? Keep climbing—and take your chances with Digger? Or face the ghost alone?

If you keep climbing, turn to PAGE 11.
If you face the ghost alone, turn to PAGE 38.

The Luckmeyer twins? What are they up to now? you wonder.

As MacFarling drives off, you notice that the sky is growing dark. Night is falling and there's a thin wispy ring of clouds around the moon.

An owl hoots near by. Then it swoops towards you! Its claws seem to be aiming right for your face!

You duck—and feel the tip of its wing brush past your cheek. When you glance up, you notice a curtain moving in a window on the first floor of your grandmother's house.

There they are! That teenage ghost and his twin sister with the braids wrapped around her head—Jane and John Luckmeyer! John points down at you and laughs evilly.

I hope *he's* not the Keeper of the Sword, you think.

Then you notice something strange up in the attic window. A light flickers on and off. On and off. Someone is up there. Is it the Keeper of the Sword?

There's only one way to find out. You take a deep breath and head towards the house. The haunted house.

If you think John Luckmeyer is the Keeper of the Sword, turn to PAGE 88.

If you think the Keeper of the Sword is hiding in the attic, turn to PAGE 102.

When the dust settles, you are stunned by what you see. Glory, the ghost stallion, has doubled in size!

And he was already a big horse.

"Neat trick," your grandmother says. "That's quite a gadget." She gets up and heads for the kitchen. "I'm going for a Coke," she tells you. "Want one?"

"N-n-no th-thanks," you stammer. You stare at Glory. The giant horse towers over you, pawing the rug.

"What button did you push?" you shout to your grandmother.

"Oh, I don't know," she calls back. "I think it was the one that turns up the sound."

Okay, you think. Maybe if I turn the sound *down* . . .

Your finger hovers over the volume button. You hesitate. What if pushing the button makes the horse bigger? What if more ghost-horses appear?

Got a better idea?

You push the volume button. *Down*.

Push the button on PAGE 5.

10

You don't exactly feel like practising the piano right now. But you decide to be nice to this old woman. You go with her, and she leads you to a fancy old grand piano.

She sits you down and turns on a metronome. *TICK. TOCK. TICK. TOCK.*

"Now play a G-major scale for me," she says.

For the next half hour, you have a piano lesson. With a ghost! When you've finished, Mrs Hatfield smiles.

"Remember how I always used to give you a treat at the end of your lesson?" she says. "Well, I have a treat for you now."

"What's this?" you ask as she hands you a piece of paper.

"It's a map of my back garden," she says. "You see, I buried a lot of gold out under the apple tree. And I forgot to mention it in my will. So no one knows it's there. I want you to have it— as a reward for being so nice to me today. For letting me give you a piano lesson one more time."

"Uh, bu-duh ... but ... wow, thanks!" you mumble like an idiot.

Then it hits you. What good will the gold do you—if you're a ghost?

Turn to PAGE 123.

You climb the last steps of the ladder. You reach the tree-house platform and pull yourself on to it.

"You don't give up, do you?" Digger says, sounding mildly impressed.

"Never," you say, trying to sound determined and tough.

Digger brushes his long, greasy brown hair out of his eyes. He's a thick, chunky kid with bad teeth and worse skin.

"So what do you want?" Digger asks you.

"A towel, for one thing," you say, wiping off some of the yucky gunk he dumped on your head.

Digger throws you a rag. You try to clean yourself up. Then you look Digger in the eyes.

"I need your help," you tell him. "There's a ghost who's following me around."

"A ghost?" Digger says. His face turns white and he looks around nervously. "Where?"

"I don't know," you admit. "He could be back at my house. Or he could be right here."

"*Here*?" Digger cries.

Go to PAGE 29.

12

You decide to trust this boy. He's a little weird looking, but he seems harmless. Even if he *is* a ghost.

"I'm John," the boy says. "You've got to get away from here. That closet is filled with horrible spirits. Quick—close the door and hide in the basement!"

You do as he says, slamming the closet door hard. Then you run down the stairs to the kitchen. Then into the basement.

Why down here? you wonder, as you look around at the damp, grungy old basement beneath your grandmother's house.

You've never liked this place. It's cold. It's dark. But even worse are the big, ugly crickets. They get in from outside through cracks in the basement walls. Then they hop all over the basement.

You hate them.

"Uh, how come we have to hide down here?" you ask.

That's when you realize that John isn't with you.

"John?" you call.

BAM! You whirl around and see the basement door slam shut. *CLICK*. And lock.

That ghost has locked you in!

Turn to PAGE 20.

Today is Friday.

So you think it's your lucky day, huh? You think the caretaker is going to come and get you out of that coffin?

Think again. Today is Friday the *13th*!

If you don't believe it, just look at the page number!

Sure, the caretaker comes. But he has an ear infection. He can't hear you screaming. And by the time he comes again next week, you're not screaming any more.

Sorry. Guess this wasn't your lucky day after all!

THE END

14

Congratulations! You picked the right Sarah. Sarah McGinnis. Born in 1918. Died in 1940, at the age of twenty-two.

You knew she was the right one—because the fencing ghost was a young beauty. So she must have died young. The other Sarah in the graveyard lived to be seventy-five years old.

Very clever of you to work it out!

Suddenly, you hear her voice. It fills your ears. "I am the Keeper of the Sword," she calls to you from her grave. "Let my foil do the work. Let go!"

Let go? Weird, you think. But you do it.

As soon as the foil leaves your hand, it floats in mid-air. Then it plunges itself deeply into the earth.

Into Brandon Estep's grave!

"Aaaaahhh!" the ghost cries. His shimmering body begins to fade—and then disappears back into the earth.

Your eyes open wide and your mouth drops open as you gaze at an amazing sight. The coffins are creeping again—back to their original positions! You did it! The curse has been defeated!

But there's only one problem. Brandon's ghostly body has gone—but his iron fist is still clutching your arm!

Turn to PAGE 86.

"Turn off that stupid light," Elvira screams. "I'm trying to get some sleep!"

"Sorry!" You quickly flick off the light. But you don't have any trouble seeing Elvira. She glows in the dark.

"I have to ask you something," you tell her.

But she pulls the pillow over her face. This isn't going to be easy. She's one sleepy ghost.

Then you have an idea. You flick on the light again. Elvira sits straight up and lets out a piercing wail.

"Elvira," you say, "I'll turn off the light if you'll answer one teeny question. Then you can sleep as long as you want. I promise."

Her eyes begin to glow green again. But she looks very sleepy. Maybe she'll be too tired to hurt you.

"Who's the most powerful ghost in the grave-yard?" you blurt out.

Elvira blinks a bit. "Hmmm," she says. "I'd say Melvin Estep's boy. He does tend to rule us with an iron hand."

"The Estep boy?" you mutter. "But there are two of them. Melvin II and Brandon. Which one?"

But Elvira doesn't answer. She's fast asleep.

And you promised you wouldn't wake her up again!

You always keep a promise. Hurry to PAGE 43.

A ghost-hunter. That is *exactly* what you need!

But how are you going to find this MacFarling person?

You dash out of your room and run downstairs as fast as you can. You rush back into the kitchen.

"Grandma," you gasp, almost out of breath. "Do you know someone called MacFarling?"

"Oh, don't go talking to me about Mac Mac-Farling," she says. "That loony. He came round here last month. Told me he thought my house would be haunted soon. Said something about a curse, too. Can you imagine that? I don't want you going anywhere *near* that man."

Uh, let's face it. Granny's not going to be much help.

So you race into the hall where she keeps her telephone books. You flip through the yellow pages. On a hunch, you look up "Ghosts".

Bingo! There he is—under "Ghost Exterminations".

Mac MacFarling. Ghost-hunter. There may be hope after all.

As long as you can get out of the house before Elvira finds out what you're doing!

Shhhh. Tiptoe out of the door to PAGE 33.

"Aaaahhhh!" you scream as you feel yourself being pulled into the ground.

You can't believe it, but it's true. Somehow, magically, you are being pulled underground, as if your own body were made of filmy air, like the ghost's.

It hurts. In fact, your whole body aches as it is dragged right into the ground. But only for an instant. Then you feel nothing.

You close your eyes. When you open them, you're lying in a coffin—on top of a pile of old rotted clothes and bones!

Your heart starts pounding wildly. You want to scream, but you don't dare. You can already sense that the coffin has very little air.

And you don't dare use it up. Not when you know that you're in an old coffin . . . two metres underground . . . with no way out.

You've been buried alive!

Go on to PAGE 40.

"Uh, I'm g-going out-outside," you stutter.

"That's nice," your grandmother says, returning to her baking. "And when you come back in, I hope you'll stop being so silly."

She still doesn't notice the ghost in the doorway.

You back away towards the door to the porch. You keep your eye on the ghost the whole time. And she keeps her glowing eyes on you. As soon as your hand reaches the doorknob behind you, you turn, fling open the door and bolt.

But just as you start down the back porch steps, two hands grab your ankle.

"Aaaahhhh!" you cry as you trip. You sprawl head first down the stairs.

Land on PAGE 39.

It's pitch-black in the house. But you're okay. You're not completely freaked out by the dark. Not yet, anyway.

"I mean it!" Lark yells. "You two are going to get it if you don't turn those lights back on. And I mean now!"

You and Robin stand frozen in the kitchen. But before you can even move towards the circuit-breaker box, the lights pop back on.

"Whoa! Oh, man!" you hear Lark and his friends yelling.

You hurry to the living-room. That's where Lark and his buddies were watching a film on TV. You peek in the door.

What a sight! Popcorn all over the floor. Drinks spilled on the rug. Sofa cushions thrown all over the room.

Lark spots you in the doorway. He glares at you and Robin—then lunges towards you. His hands reach straight for your throat.

You'd better run—quick!—to PAGE 6.

"Help!" you cry. "Let me out!"

You turn to see if there's another way out of the basement. Ugh! Those disgusting crickets are hopping everywhere. There must be hundreds of them! The chirping is enough to make you crazy.

They hop from the window-sills. They jump up and down the stairs. They pounce from the sink to the floor. From the floor to a chair. Jump! Jump! Jump!

Ack! One lands on your head!

"Yuck!" you scream. You swipe at your head. "Get off me!" More greenish-brown crickets hop around your feet.

You bang on the basement door. "Let me out of here!"

"Heh, heh," you hear John sniggering on the other side.

What a creep, you think.

Then it dawns on you.

"Hey, John," you call through the door. "What's your last name?"

"Luckmeyer," the ghost answers.

Figures! Mac MacFarling was right.

"Uh-oh," John Luckmeyer mumbles on the other side of the basement door. "Here comes trouble!"

What now! You have enough trouble already—in the form of a teenage ghoul.

Go to PAGE 68.

You try to grab her sword. But you get a handful of nothing. The sword has no substance. It isn't solid. It's just air!

The woman laughs. How can she do that without a head? "My sword is nothing without me," she says mysteriously. "And I am nothing without my head. If you want the sword, you must find my head."

You heard the woman.

Well, what are you waiting for?

Go and find her head.

Now!

Turn to PAGE 62.

The ghost floats towards you and sneers in your face.

"Do I take it that you're finally ready to make a deal?" the ghost asks.

Robin stares open-mouthed at the ghost. This is the first time he's actually seen the ghost in the flesh. Or rather, *almost* flesh.

For a moment, Robin can't speak. He just watches the airy creature floating around under the street-lamp light. Then Robin starts to smile. "Cool!" Robin says. "Really cool!"

"You want my services," the ghost goes on, "to scare those boys. And in exchange, I want your promise. You must agree to do anything I ask of you tomorrow."

"Deal!" Robin says.

"Uh, I don't know," you reply. "What if he asks us to do something wrong? Something illegal or something?"

Robin shakes his head and leans over to you. "Then we just won't do it," he whispers. "Come on. Don't you want to get back at Lark?"

Well? Don't you?

If you make the deal with the ghost, turn to PAGE 81.

If you still refuse, turn to PAGE 63.

Good work! You added right. The numbers in the date of Sarah Grayson's death add up to 23.

But there's just one problem. A big one. You've got the wrong Sarah!

Work it out. Sarah Grayson was born in 1820. She died in 1895. That made her seventy-five years old when she died.

But the ghost you saw—the fencing woman—was young. Remember? Long black hair. Ruby lips.

Not an old lady. A young one.

Which means, the Most Powerful Ghost has you in his powerful iron grip. And you've got no magical number to get out of it!

Uh-oh.

Okay. You'll get a break this time.

Go back to the graveyard and pick again. Choose the younger Sarah this time. Add up the digits in the year of her death. Then turn to that page.

Revisit the graveyard on PAGE 96.

The Civil War soldier raises his huge sword. You quickly roll out of the way. The sword plunges into the ground. You scramble to your feet and run as the soldier wrestles the blade out of the dirt.

Where can you go? What can you do? Your heart pounds as you race down the road towards town. Maybe you can get help. Maybe the police will drive by. Maybe someone besides you will see this Civil War soldier and do something to save you!

Maybe not.

You see two choices up ahead. There's a small bridge that crosses a narrow river. If you run to the bridge, maybe you can hide under it.

You also see a small red barn across the street. It's behind the farmhouse opposite your grandmother's house.

Another good hiding-place.

Which is it? The bridge or the barn?

If you run to the bridge, turn to PAGE 32.
If you hide in the barn, turn to PAGE 55.

"Why are you here?" you ask the ghost.

But your grandmother thinks you are talking to *her*.

"You know why I'm here," your grandmother answers. "I *live* here. Don't be such a goose!"

For some reason, your grandmother can't see Elvira.

You've always wanted to have a special skill. But ghost-spotting wasn't what you had in mind!

You try to think of a way to ask Elvira a question without having your grandmother think you're completely crazy. But you can't. So you keep staring at the ghost.

She glares at you a moment, then motions for you to follow her. You watch as she floats into the hall and up the stairs towards your room.

Follow a ghost? you think. Are you nuts?

Just the *idea* gives you a chill.

If you follow the ghost, turn to PAGE 49.

If you race out of this house fast—and GO HOME!—turn to PAGE 30.

You're going to trust a ghost? No way! Who knows what he's got up his ruffled sleeve? If this ghost doesn't want you to see what's in the closet, you bet it's something that can help you un-haunt your grandmother's house.

You peer into the dark closet. You can't see anything.

You glance back at the ghost. He seems nervous. Good.

So you walk right into the closet.

AAAAAAhhhhhh!!!!!

There is nothing under your feet but air! You desperately try to grab hold of something—anything!—but it's no use. You're falling down, down, down into the darkness.

See, your grandmother has turned this closet into a clothes chute. She opens the door and throws her dirty laundry in. The clothes fall straight down to the basement. That's where the washer is.

And it's a two-storey drop.

Get the picture?

Now—how would you like to be washed? Hot water or cold? With or without bleach? Because it's time to clean up your act, kid. You're all washed up in the ghost-hunting business!

THE END

You plunge your sword into Melvin Estep II's grave.

The moment the foil pierces the ground, Melvin Estep II rises up out of the earth.

Oooooohh . . . really bad choice!

He's not the MPG—he's the MHG! The Most Horrible Ghost!

As the stinking mist that surrounds him begins to clear, you can see he has no face. There is just a skull—filled with rats! The squealing rodents pop out of his eye sockets. They run up and down his cheek bones, and in through his grinning mouth.

He rises up, up, up, towering over you. He's huge! You sink to your knees in terror. "N-n-nooooo," you whimper.

He is covered in shredded rags, teeming with insects. Strips of rotting flesh fall from his skeletal body. He lifts his horrible skull head to the sky and lets out an unearthly moan. Then he fixes his rat-filled eye sockets on you!

And then . . . and then . . . his bloody hands reach for your throat!

Face it. What happens next is too disgusting, even for you!

You'd better close the book for now, and open it again when you think you can survive all the way to

THE END.

You decide to play it safe—by asking Elvira for help.

You turn and race into the house. Your grandmother is watching TV in the study. You dash past her. She doesn't even look up from her programme. The eerie light from the television is the only light in the whole house.

You hurry up the back stairs to your room. You've got to find the MPG. And there's only one person—or ghost—who might be able to help you.

You flip on a light in your small guest bedroom.

A piercing shriek shatters the night!

Now what? Cover your ears and turn to PAGE 15.

As soon as Digger hears that the ghost may be near by, he panics.

He grabs a rope that's tied around a big branch, runs to the edge of the platform and jumps. He swings down to the ground in a speedy escape.

Then he runs into his house and locks the door.

Locks the door? Against a ghost?

How silly.

You'd laugh—if you weren't still all sticky from the egg-yuck he poured on you.

Oh, well. Like most bullies, Digger turned out to be a coward.

So much for asking your worst enemy for help.

Stick to your best friend from now on.

Your best friend is waiting for you on PAGE 73.

You decide to get out of your grandmother's house. On the double.

"Uh, Grandma," you say. "I don't feel well. In fact, I think I'm getting really ill. I think I should go home."

"But dear," your grandmother says. "You *can't* go home. Not with your parents away on holiday."

Well, it was worth a try.

You swallow hard and glance over to where the ghost was standing. She's gone.

Maybe you were imagining things. Maybe the gravestones *aren't* moving. Maybe you really *are* ill!

The best thing to do is go up to your room and lie down. You climb the stairs to the first floor. But as you reach the door to your room, you freeze.

There in the doorway is a terrifying sight!

Hurry to PAGE 42.

Your throat tightens in terror. Your heart pounds wildly. Both you *and* your grandmother are cursed, now!

Your granny can't even *see* the ghosts! She won't be able to save herself. It's all up to you.

You grip the sword so hard your hand cramps. You've got to stop the coffins from moving again. And you've got to do it now, before the final coffin moves into place and the curse is complete!

But who is the Most Powerful Ghost?

"One more letter," you mutter. Only one more letter is needed to spell out the message. The last letter in the word DIE—the letter E.

Then it hits you. The Most Powerful Ghost must be someone whose last name starts with an E!

That's it! You may live after all! You run through the graveyard, looking at the tomb-stones, searching for E's.

You find three. Melvin Estep. Melvin Estep II. And Brandon Estep.

But which one is the MPG?

You could guess. Or you could go into the house and ask Elvira for help.

If you guess—take a stab at it on PAGE 48.
If you ask Elvira for help, turn to PAGE 28.

The bridge looks good to you. You can slip down the bank to the river and hide under it. You might be able to sneak round and change direction. Maybe you'll lose the soldier after all.

But before you even reach the river-bank, you feel a heavy hand on your shoulder.

"Halt, traitor!" the soldier cries.

"No!" you scream, twisting away. You stumble a bit and lurch forward, out of his grasp. You keep running.

Finally you reach the bridge. But the soldier is right behind you. He swings his sword wildly at you—as if to cut off your head!

"No!" you cry again, jumping backwards.

Uh-oh. Backwards wasn't a good idea. You've just leapt off the bridge!

And it's a long way down. Oooh. That hurt.

You have a fifty-fifty chance of surviving that fall.

Remember what page you're on—PAGE 32. Then throw this book up in the air.

If it lands with the front cover facing up, turn to PAGE 105.

If it lands with the cover face down, turn to PAGE 69.

Luckily, everything in your grandma's small town is within biking distance. Twenty minutes later, you've biked over to Mac MacFarling's office. Which happens to be located in his garage.

You knock on the side door of the garage.

"Come in!" a voice calls. You yank open the door.

Wow! you think when you see him.

Mac MacFarling has frizzy, kinky blond hair sticking out all over his head. He's wearing six earrings, a nose ring and a pair of heavy black-framed glasses with blue lenses in them. He's about 20 years old.

So that's why your grandma didn't like him. He's cool!

"What's up?" MacFarling asks. "You look like you've just seen a ghost." He laughs. "Sorry. Just a little ghost-hunting humour."

You explain about Elvira, and that she told you the ghosts are going to take over your grandmother's house.

"I've been expecting this," MacFarling says, shaking his head. "I tried to warn your grandmother."

"Can you help us?" you plead. His eyes are hidden behind the blue lenses. You can't tell what he's thinking.

Will Mac MacFarling help you?

Find out on PAGE 37.

You run over to Melvin Estep's grave and plunge your sword into the ground.

And wait.

Nothing happens.

Does that mean you've actually done it? Did you put an end to the curse of the creeping coffins?

You step back from the grave, leaving the sword standing straight up from the dirt. You take a deep breath. Could it really all be over?

Suddenly, one of the other two coffins—one of the other Esteps!—starts to move!

Oh, no! You chose the wrong Estep!

It's all over, all right. All over for YOU!

Before your astonished eyes, the headstone creeps across the graveyard. Within seconds, it reaches the third row. When the headstone stops creeping, the word DIE is complete.

And so is your adventure in this book. Complete. Finished. Done. As in . . .

THE END

PS Here's a hint. Next time you try to defeat the creeping coffins, ask Elvira for help. Don't leave so much to chance!

"Help!" Robin screams as the knife drifts towards him.

Oh, no! Right beside the floating knife is the ghost-boy.

You grab the baseball bat and take a swing.

The bat goes right through the ghost's see-through body. He laughs as if you had tickled him.

Unfortunately, the bat comes out on the other side of him and smashes right into Robin's desk lamp.

Oooops.

The lamp flies off the desk and smashes on to the floor.

"What was that?" a woman's voice calls from the hallway.

Uh-oh. Robin's mum is on the way.

Turn to PAGE 75.

You hear a booming *CRACK*! In the next instant, the ghost of Brandon Estep rises up out of his grave.

Is he the MPG? Have you chosen the right Estep?

You peer at Brandon as he floats towards you. Hc's a young man wearing a black leather motor-cycle jacket. With heavy metal spikes and chains. And a metal hand.

A metal hand?

A chill of terror runs through you. This must be him. The Most Powerful Ghost. The ghost with the iron hand.

You raise the foil again. But the ghost lunges at you—and grabs your arm with his iron hand.

Your arm freezes. You can't move!

For a moment, you panic. Then you remember what MacFarling told you. The date of Sarah's death. It's magic, somehow.

Did you write down the date like MacFarling told you? Good. Then find the date and add up all four digits in the year. What's the new number? Well, that's your next page number. Turn to that page.

You don't remember the date? Turn to PAGE 96 and choose one of the Sarahs. Add up the digits in the year of her death and turn to that page.

Suddenly, MacFarling swings into gear. He picks up a strange electronic box and heads for the door. "Come on," he says. "We've got to hurry. Let's go!"

Finally—someone who can help you! You feel better already.

MacFarling jumps into his car—an old VW Beetle. You hop on your bike. As you ride to your grandmother's house, he drives along beside you. He rolls down the window and talks to you the whole time.

"Have the gravestones been moving around?" he asks.

"Yes!" you exclaim. So, you're *not* crazy! "Why are they doing that?"

"I'm not sure," he says. "I've only seen it once before. But I think they're moving into position to spell out some kind of message—or curse."

Graves can spell? That doesn't sound possible. But you're ready to believe anything now. "How can we stop them?" you ask Mac.

"It won't be easy," he tells you.

You were afraid of that.

Turn to PAGE 45.

Forget this, you decide. Digger is too much of a jerk. You'd rather face the ghost alone.

You climb down the ladder and start to head back home. Pretty soon, you realize that someone is walking beside you. You can hear his footsteps. You can feel the air moving, where he's swinging his arm. You just can't see him.

It must be the ghost!

"Leave me alone!" you shout at him, although you can't see a thing.

"Heh, heh," he laughs under his breath. "You'll never get away from me."

Oh, yeah? you think. We'll see about that.

Try to lose this bloke on PAGE 79.

OUCH.

You land face down at the bottom of the steps.

Good thing it wasn't a long flight of stairs. You're only bruised and scratched. You've scraped your chin, but nothing's broken.

"Ha, ha, ha!" you hear a boy's voice say.

You turn towards the voice. You want to see the jerk who made you trip.

Hey—wait a minute.

There *is* no jerk behind you. You blink to be sure.

Yes. You're sure.

There's absolutely *no one* standing at the top of the stairs! Or anywhere else!

Turn to PAGE 44.

You start to panic. The coffin feels—crowded. You try to sit up, but you bump your head. Ouch.

Uh-oh. Was that . . . something moving?

What is it? you wonder. Your heart races. Snakes? Worms? Rats?

Something bumps your knee. You start banging on the coffin lid, trying to get out.

"Hey—hold still," a voice says.

Slowly, the ghost-boy begins to materialize. He is squeezed in beside you. The coffin is so crowded now, you can hardly move.

"Take my hand," the ghost-boy says. "Time to continue the journey."

You stare at the ghost's outstretched hand.

If you take the ghost-boy's hand, go to PAGE 82.

If you don't, turn to PAGE 98.

Your stomach turns at the sight of her bloody neck. Then you notice the ghost's body is still hovering below you. It floats up the steps and somehow attaches to her head.

"Thank you," she says once she's in one piece. She hands you her foil. "I am the Keeper of the Sword. Take this—and use it as you will. Now I must return to my grave."

You remember Mac MacFarling's instructions. "Wait!" you call. "What's your name?"

"Sarah," she whispers as her form fades away. Then she's gone.

You run to the phone and dial MacFarling's number. When he answers, you tell him you've got the sword.

"Good," MacFarling says. "Listen carefully. Find her grave in the graveyard. Write down the year of her death. It's a special number. You'll need it. Then plunge her sword into the grave of the MPG. That's the only way to keep the graves from spelling out the curse."

"But how do I find the MPG?" you ask.

"Oops," MacFarling says. "Call waiting. Got to go!"

He hangs up. Call waiting? you think. What a liar! He just doesn't know how to help you find the MPG. Now what?

If you go to the graveyard, turn to PAGE 96.
If you think the MPG will come to you, turn to PAGE 125.

42

A ghost fills the doorway. But this ghost isn't just a filmy version of a live human being. This ghost isn't like Elvira Martin.

This ghost is hideous! His whole face is greyish-blue. His tongue and eyes bulge out. He looks as if he died while being choked. Then his blueish hands reach out for you.

That does it. No way are you staying in this creepy haunted house for another minute!

You run back downstairs to your grandmother. You beg. You plead. You cry. Then you pull out every trick in the book. Even the one where you fake a high fever by putting the thermometer on a light bulb.

Eventually, your grandmother gives in. She calls your parents. They cut short their holiday, pick you up and take you home. They're pretty angry with you. But you don't care. At least you've got away from that haunted house!

You flop down on the bed in your room. That's when you feel something poking you. Something in your bed!

You sit up and stare at your blanket.

It's sliding around on the bed—all by itself!

Slide over to PAGE 61.

You turn and run out of the room, leaving Elvira snoring peacefully in your bed.

You head back to the graveyard. You're going to have to take a chance on one of the Estep boys. And fast! Before the graves move again.

Only one letter left before the curse is complete. That's what keeps going through your head.

When you reach the graveyard you are almost out of breath from running up and down the stairs so many times. But the sight that greets you nearly takes your breath away completely. You think you might faint.

The graveyard is filled with ghosts! Horrible ghosts. One of them—an old man with long, stringy hair—carries an axe. A woman sobs. A head without a body passes, then a body without a head. Each ghost is worse than the last!

Then you remember the fencing foil in your hands. You raise the sword to fend them off. It works. They float all round the graveyard, but they don't come near you.

You run straight for the Estep graves.

But which one? Melvin II or Brandon?

You've got to choose.

If you pick Melvin Estep II, turn to PAGE 27.
If you pick Brandon Estep, turn to PAGE 47.

44

"Ha, ha," the boy's voice taunts again.

"Gotcha!" a girl's voice joins in.

Right in front of your amazed eyes, a boy and a girl slowly begin to materialize.

When they finally take shape, you can see that they're teenagers. But teenagers from a long time ago. The boy is dressed in a funny-looking black suit with a frilly white shirt and shiny black shoes. The girl is wearing a long, old-fashioned white linen dress. Her hair is braided and the braids are wrapped around her head three times.

The boy and girl look almost solid—but not quite. You can see right through them.

"Boo!" they shout at the same time. Then they double over with hysterical laughter.

Your heart is still pounding wildly.

Is this really happening? Or are you dreaming?

There's one way to find out. Pinch yourself.
If it hurts, turn to PAGE 53.
If it doesn't, turn to PAGE 60.

"First," MacFarling explains, "you'll have to fight the Keeper of the Sword. That's one of the ghosts. You need to get the special sword—and use it to stop the MPG."

"What's the MPG?" you ask.

"The Most Powerful Ghost," MacFarling says. "It's a term for the spirit who has control over a graveyard.

"Once you have the sword," Mac continues, "you must plunge it into the grave of the MPG. But you've got to hurry! Because when all the graves have moved into position and spell out the message—it'll be too late! The curse will be complete. And after that, you'll *never* be able to get the ghosts back into their graves."

Your head is spinning from what Mac's just told you. But you nod as if you understand.

You've arrived at your grandmother's house. MacFarling stops his car and hops out. You get off your bike and park it. MacFarling faces your grandmother's house and switches on the funky electronic box he's carrying. Red dials light up. Then you hear a loud beeping sound.

"Uh-oh," MacFarling says. "Major trouble. Give me a dollar."

If you give MacFarling a dollar, turn to PAGE 57.

If you refuse to give him money, turn to PAGE 74.

46

The knife floats towards you and Robin. Quickly you grab the needle-point pillow. You hold it in front of you like a shield.

Are you crazy? You're going to use *that* pillow? The one Robin's mother lovingly needle-pointed for him? The one that took her seventy-four hours of finger-aching work to complete? You're using it to block an attack from a flying *knife*?

Oh, dear. We're talking serious bad judgement here.

The pillow, of course, is ripped to shreds. But that's just the beginning. Just the first of many bad decisions you make in your life. For instance:

A few weeks later, you're at a picnic. You drop a blueberry muffin on to a big red anthill. The fire ants swarm all over the muffin. You decide to pick it up and eat it anyway.

Your mother gives you a hundred dollars for your birthday. A beggar asks you for a quarter, but you don't have any change. You tear off a piece of the hundred-dollar bill and give it to him instead.

When you grow up, you win a TV game show. The prize is a new car! But the car is blue, and you hate the colour. So you say "No thanks," and give it back.

See the problem? Of course none of this will happen—*if* you can learn how to choose more carefully.

Go to PAGE 100 and choose again.

You cross your fingers and decide to take a chance on Brandon Estep. You run over to his tombstone and stand in front of it.

You hold the sword in both hands like a dagger, with the point down. Your hands tremble so much you're afraid you'll drop the sword. You tighten your grip and take a deep breath.

Then you raise the sword above Brandon's grave and prepare to plunge it into the ground.

But something stops you.

What happened? Find out on PAGE 36.

48

Time is running out. That last coffin could creep into place before you even cross over to a grave! Then it will be all over. For you *and* your grandmother.

You are too terrified to think.

So you decide to guess.

Well ... what are you waiting for? Go ahead and guess.

Which one is the Most Powerful Ghost?

Melvin Estep? Melvin Estep II? Or Brandon Estep?

If you pick Melvin Estep, turn to PAGE 34.
If you pick Melvin Estep II, turn to PAGE 27.
If you pick Brandon Estep, turn to PAGE 47.

You follow Elvira to your room on the first floor. The moment you step into the bedroom, she slams the door.

Then she whirls around to face you. Her eyes turn green and begin to glow.

You back away, stumbling, and fall on to the bed.

"You little wretch," she says. "I don't want any trouble from you!" Sparks seem to fly from her flashing green eyes. You shrink back into the pillows.

Then Elvira gazes around the room. "Yes, yes," she says. "This will do nicely."

"Wh-what do you mean?" you stammer.

Elvira floats towards the bed. She hovers over you. "I'm taking over this room, now," she tells you. "Get out!"

You would love to leave, but you are shaking too hard to get up. Besides, you have to find out what's going on! Elvira is the only one who can explain it to you.

"Please," you beg, "just tell me why you are here. And why are the graves moving?"

"Shut up!" she screeches. "And get off that bed. I want to lie down! I haven't slept in a bed in fifty-one years!"

Uh-oh, you realize. You aren't just dealing with a ghost here. You're dealing with a ghost in a very bad mood!

You'd better do what she says on PAGE 72.

The next day, you and Robin meet right after breakfast. The ghost shows up an hour later. Right on time.

"Okay," the ghost says. "Here's the deal. I want you to eat a plateful of worms."

"Are you kidding?" Robin blurts out.

"Nope," the ghost says. "You've got to eat worms. Stay here. I'll get them."

The ghost's body suddenly forms into a funnel shape and disappears into the ground in Robin's front garden. He looks like a human tornado vanishing into the earth.

When he zooms back up, the ghost has a handful of worms.

He walks over to Robin's front porch. Sitting on the steps is a small plate.

"Eat these," the ghost says, dumping the worms on the plate.

"Yuck!" Robin says. "No way!"

"If you don't," the ghost says, "I'll haunt you for the rest of your life. Like this." The ghost makes himself into an airy tornado again. But this time, the funnel flows into Robin's head. It goes in one ear—and out the other!

"Yeow!" Robin screams. "Okay! Okay! I'll eat them!"

Turn to PAGE 109.

You stare at the glowing ghostly face. Your mouth drops open as the face rises out of the moose head. The woman's face floats up and hangs in mid-air, right in front of you.

"Thank you," the head says. "You have released me from my trap."

Her eyes are large and bright blue. Her ruby lips shimmer in the darkness. Her long black hair hangs down, falling below her neck.

Her neck? You glance at it—and try not to scream.

Torn flesh dangles from the bottom of her neck. Blood drips from the ragged edges.

Suddenly you realize what you're seeing. It looks as if her head has been chopped off!

Try not to faint. Turn to PAGE 41.

"Okay," you say to the ghost. "I'll do anything. Just help us!"

"Good," the ghost-boy answers.

An instant later, you hear Lark go flying to the floor.

"Yeow!" Lark yells as he hits the rug hard.

You and Robin stop running. You turn and laugh.

"Stop sniggering, you little twerps," Lark snarls as he clambers to his feet. "You're dead meat."

He comes towards you and Robin, one hand clenched in a fist. The ghost-boy winks, and the rug flies out from under Lark. He sprawls on the floor again.

You and Robin laugh so hard you double over.

For the rest of the night, every time Lark or one of his buddies tries to come after you, the ghost pulls a prank. Nothing big. Nothing that would make Lark suspect anything. Just enough to keep them from bothering you.

You and Robin sleep very peacefully that night.

The next morning, when you get home, the ghost is in your room, waiting for you. "Okay," the ghost says. "Time to keep your promise. Let's go."

Go? Go where?

Find out on PAGE 84.

No doubt about it. You are definitely awake. This is really happening. Which means you are face to face with two teenage ghosts.

You stand up and brush yourself off.

"Who are you?" you ask, trying not to let your voice tremble. "What do you want? What are you doing here?"

"I'm Jane Luckmeyer," the girl ghost says. "And this is my dearly beloved twin brother, John."

John bows deeply. Then he sticks out his tongue.

"Oh, John," Jane cries. "This will be so much fun!"

"Yes, dear sister," John answers. "We haven't had anyone to torment in ages."

"An eternity!" Jane agrees. "But I've spent the time thinking of ever more horrible tricks and tortures."

You don't like the sound of that! Could these two creeps have something to do with the creeping coffins?

"Tell me something," you say, hoping you sound casual. "Why have the coffins been moving around?"

But the twins don't answer you. Instead, they cackle horribly and grin at you.

Go on to PAGE 66.

You start to swing the rope, hoping to lasso the wild ghost stallion.

Are you kidding?

Do you know how long it takes to learn how to lasso?

And you don't even have that rope tied in the right kind of knot, do you?

Admit it. Unless you've grown up on a dude ranch or within two hundred miles of a pack of wild stallions, you don't have a flat chance of lassoing this crazed animal.

So . . .

If you were born in Colorado, Montana or Wyoming, turn to PAGE 58.

If you were born anywhere else, turn to PAGE 94.

You race across the lawn and over the hill to the small barn. You swing open the door.

Instantly, more than forty chickens flap down out of the rafters at you! Feathers fly everywhere.

"Aaaaa-choooo!" The feathers tickle your nose. They get in your mouth. You swipe at the downy tufts.

The clucking is so loud you cover your ears. Then you cover your *head*. "Aaaaaahhhh!" you scream. The chickens are swooping towards your hair.

Huh?

Why are they swooping towards your hair? You've heard that *bats* will fly at people and get tangled in their hair. But chickens?

There's definitely something weird going on with these birds.

Turn to PAGE 97.

56

You decide to ask your worst enemy to help you.

Digger Sukowski.

That's the first name that pops into your head when you think about how to deal with this ghost.

Digger is a sixth-grader who lives a few blocks away. He's a bully and a jerk, and you can't think of anyone meaner or tougher. Perfect.

"Uh, wait right here," you tell the ghost.

You dash out of the house and run all the way to Digger's back garden. That's where Digger and his friends have built a tree house.

The ladder leading up to the tree house has a sign on it.

NO TRESPASSERS. THIS MEANS YOU. CLIMB THIS LADDER AT YOUR OWN RISK!

You swallow hard and put your foot on the ladder.

Keep climbing on PAGE 70.

You reluctantly hand MacFarling a dollar bill.

He folds the dollar in half twice. Then he jams it into a tiny slot of his electronic box. A minute later, the beeping stops. The box spits the dollar back out.

"Thanks," MacFarling says. "The spirit counter was jammed." He gives the dollar back to you.

Weird, you think. But it seems to have worked.

Then, MacFarling stares at the red dials on his machine.

"Bad news, kid," MacFarling says at last. "By my count, there are ten ghosts in the house already. That's way over my limit. You're on your own."

He starts back towards his car.

"Wait!" you call after him. "You can't leave me here! Please! You have to help me!"

MacFarling hesitates for a minute. Then he shrugs. "Okay," he says. "This what I'm willing to do. I'll help you make a map of the graveyard. Come on."

A map of the graveyard? What for? you wonder.

But you don't ask questions. You just follow Mac into the cemetery and do what he tells you. An hour later, you've got a drawing of the first four rows of gravestones.

To see the map, turn to PAGE 127.

Whoosh! The rope snaps through the air with a swish! It flutters over Glory's head. The ghost-stallion rears up with an angry whinny. You flick your wrist and give the rope a sharp yank. Bingo! You did it.

Talk about heavy-duty lassoing!

Glory snorts and stamps his hooves, nearly lifting you off the ground. But you hang on. Using all your strength, you drag the ghost-horse down the stairs. You pull him into the study, where your grandmother is watching television.

"Grandma! Look!" you shout. "I've roped a *ghost*-horse!"

Your grandmother gazes up from her television programme and gives you a warm smile. Then she eyes the ghost-horse.

"Now, don't expect me to fall for that," she says. "I know all about the gizmos you kids have these days. What is that? Some kind of hologram? Or video game? See, I'm up to date."

Hologram? Video game? Is she nuts?

With a twinkle in her eye, your grandmother reaches for the TV remote control—and aims it at the horse.

She pushes a button.

Showers of sparks shoot out of the remote. A cracking *BOOM* shakes the house.

What has your grandmother done?

Find out on PAGE 9.

"No way," you say. "I'm not making a deal with a ghost!"

"Fine," the ghost-boy says. "You're on your own!" He vanishes.

Maybe this wasn't such a great idea.

Lark and his friends catch up with you easily. What happens next isn't pretty. By the time Lark and his friends have finished, you and Robin are a mess.

You're lying on the damp grass in Robin's front garden. You're bruised from being tackled. Your T-shirt and jeans are grass-stained. Your hair is a tangled nest. Lark used both sets of knuckles to give you "noogies".

"Oooh," Robin fumes. "I could strangle him!"

"No, you couldn't," you reply. "You're not big enough. In fact, he strangled us."

"True," Robin admits. "But we've got to do *something* to get back at him. I wish that ghost would come back. Maybe he could scare the living bazookas out of my stupid brother."

No sooner has Robin said the words than the ghost appears.

"You rang?" the ghost says with a sly smile.

Turn to PAGE 22.

60

You didn't feel that?

Uh-oh. Pinch again.

Nothing?

You've obviously fallen asleep while reading this book! You've gone bye-bye. To dreamland. You're probably snoring, too.

The thing is, in your dreams you'll probably be able to handle these ghosts.

But in real life? Well ... that's a different story.

So go ahead. Snooze on. Enjoy it.

We'll see how well you survive—when you wake up!

When you wake up, turn to PAGE 53.

Your heart races as you scoot away from the moving blanket. You press your back up against the wall. Something bumps into your foot. Then your knee.

"OW!" Something invisible pinched you!

Little by little, the "something" begins to appear.

At first, it's only a ghostly head. The head of a boy. He's about twelve years old and he's grinning at you.

"Surprise," he says as his body, arms and legs begin to materialize in front of you. He looks almost solid—but not quite.

"Who are you? Where . . . where did you come from?" you finally blurt out.

"Wouldn't you like to know?" he says. Then he floats over to the window and gestures towards your family's car in the driveway. "Bumpy ride, wasn't it?" he says with a laugh.

Bumpy ride? Oh, no! He hitched a ride with you from your grandmother's house!

You've got to do something to get rid of this ghost.

But what?

And who's going to help you?

If you choose your best friend to help you, turn to PAGE 73.

If you choose your worst enemy to help you, turn to PAGE 56.

"Okay," you tell her. "I'll find your head. Wait here."

But where should you look?

You dash up the stairs to the attic. It's the only room you haven't been in since you arrived. And you *definitely* would have noticed a head if you'd seen one.

You rummage around in the attic. You search through everything. Twice. Trunks of old clothes. Piles of old furniture. Golf clubs. No ghost-head.

You glance around the dusty room. Think! There may not be much time left. If I were a ghost-head, where would I be? you ask yourself. You suddenly spot a large moose head sitting on the floor by a broken chair.

You kneel down to examine the moth-eaten moose head. Up close, it looks even worse. The antlers are cracked and one eye is missing. It is filthy and has a musty odour.

It's not even human. But what choice do you have?

It's the only head here!

Besides—you're in a big hurry. You've got to get the sword before the coffins creep again!

You grab the moose head and race downstairs.

You only hope the Keeper of the Sword won't be furious when she sees the head you've brought her!

Cross your fingers for luck and turn to PAGE 80.

No deal, you decide. You're not going to make a bargain with a ghost.

You wouldn't even make a deal like that with your mum. Promise to do "whatever" she wants? You might end up raking leaves and washing her car for a year!

"No, thanks," you tell the ghost. "No deal. I don't make promises I can't keep."

The ghost smiles at you. A nice smile. For the first time since you met him, he seems genuinely friendly.

"That's what I wanted to hear," the ghost says. "That you wouldn't make a promise unless you really meant to keep it. I've been looking for someone honest like you for a long time."

Then the ghost reaches into his trouser pocket. He pulls out a gold coin.

"Take this," he says, handing it to you. "And promise me that you will never spend it. The coin will bring you good luck as long as you never sell it, spend it or give it away. But make sure you are not buried with the coin. Otherwise, your spirit will never rest. Like me, you'll be forced to roam the earth looking for someone to give it to."

You take the coin from him, and he sighs with relief. Then the ghost-boy vanishes completely . . . and you never see him again.

THE END

Keep away from the Luckmeyer twins. That should be easy, no problem. Twins are pretty easy to spot.

Then it hits you—do they always stick together? Are they boys or girls? And how old are they? No way to know.

Hmmmm. Maybe this will be more difficult than you thought.

You slink into your grandmother's house. You feel creepy, knowing the place is loaded with ghosts. And how are you going to find the Keeper of the Sword? You don't have a clue. Your head swims as you wander up to the first floor.

BAM! A door bangs open. It nearly hits you on the head.

You jump back, and peer into a hall closet.

"Don't go in there!" a voice behind you warns.

You whirl around and see—a ghost! A teenager from another time. He's dressed in an old-fashioned black velvet suit with a frilly white shirt. His hair is slicked back and combed neatly behind his ears. He's smiling—but it's a sneaky smile.

Should you listen to him?

If you stay out of the closet, turn to PAGE 12.
If you see what's in the closet, turn to PAGE 26.

You stare down at the map of gravestones in your hands. You wonder how it can possibly help.

"Big trouble," Mac says, peering over your shoulder. "The message is already almost completely spelled out."

"What message?" you ask, puzzled.

"Look at these first four rows," he says, pointing at the paper. "The rest of the graves don't matter. That's why I didn't put them on the map. Take a pen and circle the first letter of the last name on each tombstone. It spells out a message! Don't you see?"

No. You don't see. And you won't see—until you do it.

So do it.

Turn to the map on PAGE 127. Circle the first letter of the *last* name on each tombstone. It will spell out a message—or part of one.

When you have discovered the message, turn to PAGE 91.

66

The Luckmeyer twins float down the steps towards you. And they both have an evil glint in their eyes.

Uh-oh. These two spell trouble. *Double* trouble.

Run! you tell yourself. But which way?

If you run away from them, you'll be running straight towards the graveyard.

But your only way back into the house is by getting past the Luckmeyer twins first. They're floating closer and closer to you—and John is hiding something behind his back.

You freeze. You can't decide what to do. You know John is up to something. And you know you'd better not stick around to find out what it is! But which way should you go?

Don't think! Run!

If you run towards the graveyard, turn to PAGE 93.

If you try to slip past the twins and back into the house, turn to PAGE 108.

You're trying to crawl out from under the sink, when the lights pop back on.

A moment later, Lark and his buddies zoom into the kitchen.

"What are you two jerks doing?" Lark asks.

"Nothing," Robin says quickly.

"Yeah, nothing," you chime in.

Lark looks at his friends and they all nod. You don't like the way they're smiling at you.

Uh-oh.

Hurry back to PAGE 6.

Ick! Another cricket plops on your head.

"Let me out!" you yell again, pounding on the door.

Immediately, the door swings open.

Uh-oh. The ghost was right. Trouble *has* arrived—in a big way.

It's your grandma. And she's steaming mad.

"What in heaven's name are you up to?" your grandmother scolds.

You glance past her into the kitchen and see what she means. The whole place is a mess. Flour is scattered all over the floor. Pots and pans are stacked on the chairs and table. Every single item that was in the refrigerator is sitting on the kitchen worktop.

"What on earth have you done?" your grandmother demands, pointing at the huge mess.

Behind her back, you see the ghostly John Luckmeyer with a big grin plastered across his smirking face.

Quick—what are you going to tell her?

If you decide to make up a story, turn to PAGE 71.

If you tell the truth, turn to PAGE 112.

The book lands with the front cover down. Lucky you! You survive the fall off the bridge. But don't kid yourself. You're pretty bruised and scratched up.

"Owww . . ." you moan, as you lie on the rocky banks of the river.

Mistake. You shouldn't have moaned. Now the soldier knows where you are!

In a flash, he jumps off the bridge and towers over you.

"Prepare to die!" he shouts.

Can't this bloke think of anything else to say?

Then he . . . well . . . he . . . you know. He finishes you off with one thrust of that beautiful, mother-of-pearl-handled, sapphire-encrusted sword.

Hey—don't look so surprised.

We said there was a fifty-fifty chance of surviving the fall. We didn't say anything about surviving this book!

THE END

70

You clutch the tree-house ladder so hard you get a splinter. The ladder is nailed to the side of the tree. There isn't much space for your hands or your feet. The boards are wobbly and crooked. You don't dare look down.

When you're halfway up the ladder—too high to jump down, but not high enough to lift yourself on to the platform—Digger pops his head out of the tree house. He gives you a mean grin.

"Hey," he says in a nasty voice. "Lookee what we got here. A trespasser!"

Then he leans over the edge of the platform with a bucket in his hands. He raises the bucket, then turns it upside down.

Directly over your head.

Turn to PAGE 7.

"Uh, I was trying to make dinner for you, Grandma," you say. If you told the truth, she'd think you were lying. Then you'd be in even bigger trouble.

"Well . . ." Your grandmother's face begins to soften.

Then John Luckmeyer floats over to you. Before you realize what he's doing, John picks up one of your grandmother's best china tea-cups. He knocks it to the floor, right by your hand. The teacup lands with a horrible crash.

Oh, no!

You start to open your mouth to explain. But then another ghost appears on the other side of you. This one is a girl. She's wearing an old-fashioned, long white linen dress. Her hair is braided and the braids are wrapped around her head three times.

"Hello," she says with a snigger. "I'm Jane Luckmeyer."

Great, you think. Another one. Trapped between the Luckmeyer twins.

She picks up the china saucer that goes with the teacup John's just smashed. Then she throws it like a Frisbee across the room. Somehow she makes it look as if *you* threw it. The saucer crash-lands at your grandmother's feet.

"That's it," your grandmother says. "Go to your room!"

Turn to PAGE 124.

72

You jump up from the bed.

Elvira lies down, neatly spreading her white satin dress on the covers. Her long red hair fans out across the pillow.

"Ahhhh," she sighs. "A real bed." She shuts her eyes.

You hope she doesn't sleep too long. You have so many questions to ask. And you hope she'll be in a better mood when she wakes up!

She dozes for exactly two minutes. Then her eyes pop open. You notice they aren't glowing green any more.

"Ah," Elvira says. "That's better."

Now that she's awake, you're not sure how to begin. You're almost too freaked out to speak. But you have to know! "Why are the graves moving?" you ask. "What's going on?"

"It's the curse of the creeping coffins," the ghostly woman answers. "And we're moving into this house. All of us."

All of us?

Gulp.

What does *that* mean?

Rush to PAGE 106.

You decide you need your best friend's help. So you call Robin. He lives only two houses away.

Without even a goodbye to your mum and dad, you zoom out of the front door. You run to Robin's house as fast as you can.

"Hi!" Robin says. "That was fast. What's up?"

"You're not going to believe me," you warn him.

"Try me," Robin says, throwing three juggling balls in the air.

Robin has been trying to learn to juggle for six months. He just can't get the hang of it.

"My grandmother's house is haunted," you explain quickly. "The coffins in the graveyard behind the house were creeping around. The ghosts escaped from their graves. And—" you pause and take a deep breath. "And one of them followed me home."

Robin stares at you as if you're crazy. He lets all three balls drop to the floor with a *thud-thud-thud*.

"Yeah, sure. Right," he says sarcastically.

A moment later, all three juggling balls rise up from the floor. To your amazement, they start juggling themselves!

Then one of them flies right at Robin—and hits him in the face!

Go to PAGE 101.

Maybe your grandmother was right. Maybe he can't be trusted. Maybe he's a scam artist.

"What do you want a dollar for?" you ask him.

But before he can answer, the funky electronic box beeps one more time. Really loudly.

Then all of a sudden, a lid on top flips open— and a small plastic hand pops out!

Cool! you think. You've seen these things before.

It's a gag bank. Your uncle had one, but his used dimes. It was a small black plastic box with a slot on top, just like MacFarling's gadget. When you put a dime in the slot, a lid would fly open and a plastic hand would pop out. The hand would grab the dime and pull it into the box. It cracked you up.

But why is MacFarling playing around with a trick bank? You're supposed to be hunting ghosts.

"Give me a dollar!" Mac screams frantically.

But before you can answer him, the plastic hand reaches further out of the box—and grabs you by the throat!

In the next instant, it pulls you into the box!

You don't think your uncle's bank worked like this.

Too bad you didn't have a dollar when you needed it!

THE END

Robin's mum is furious when she sees the broken lamp.

How furious?

Let's just say you and Robin will be mowing lawns for a long time to pay for the lamp.

But the good news is, the ghost seems to have vanished! Maybe Robin's mum scared him off.

"You weren't kidding," Robin says. "There really is a ghost!"

"I tried to tell you," you say to him. "Listen, can I sleep over? The ghost is probably back at my house, just waiting to get me!"

"No problem," Robin tells you. "You'll be a lot safer here."

Don't bet on it.

Turn to PAGE 89.

"Where are we?" you ask the ghost-boy.

"Oh . . ." he says. "You know."

No, you think. I *don't*.

You pass an elaborate gold-framed mirror hanging in mid-air. You look at your reflection. And gasp!

Your legs! Your arms! They've gone! You stare at the "you" in the mirror. You can see the furniture behind you—right through your own body!

Maybe it's a trick mirror! You glance down at yourself. It's no trick. Your legs are transparent.

Your heart drops into your see-through feet as you realize the truth. You're a ghost, now, too!

Someone suddenly calls your name. You whirl around—and see your old piano teacher, Mrs Hatfield. She was a sweet old lady, about ninety years old. She died last year. You have to admit you haven't missed her much. You never liked having piano lessons.

"Oh, there you are!" Mrs Hatfield exclaims. "Come with me. I want you to play some scales."

If you go with Mrs Hatfield, turn to PAGE 10.
If you refuse, turn to PAGE 87.

It's true. Your feet have turned to stone. So has the rest of you.

Help! you want to cry out.

But you can't speak. Stone lips don't move.

"I warned you," Jane says quietly.

"Ha, ha," John says, laughing and pointing at you. "You're stuck!" He wags a finger in your stony face.

You'd like to bite him, but you can't. You can't do anything. You're a statue. You've turned to solid stone.

"See what happens when you walk among the dead?" John says. "You should have listened to Jane. Don't *ever* walk with a dead person into a graveyard. It's the most dangerous thing you can do."

Now they tell you!

Go on to PAGE 113. If you can. Go on and try it. Try to turn the page, stony-fingers!

You press the mute button. Instantly, the Neanderthal man disappears.

Phew. Close one, you think.

Then you have an idea. You press the mute button again. Yes. It works just as you thought it would. The ghost of the Neanderthal reappears. And when you press it again, he disappears. You can keep switching back and forth.

Now you see him—now you don't!

Needless to say, this is a cool toy. You and your grandmother play with it for a few days. Then you call the local newspapers. They come out and write a story about you. Pretty soon, you're famous. Every computer game company in America and Japan wants to buy your invention.

The amazing remote-controlled hologram machine!

You tell them the truth. You have no idea how it works. But for ten million dollars, they can have the remote *and* the house. And they can try to work it out for themselves.

When the deal is made, you leave the remote and the house behind you. But there is still one more "remote" in your future. A *remote* island in the South Pacific! That's where you and your grandmother fly off to. Why? Just in case the company works out you've sold them a house full of ghosts!

THE END

You take off running. Top speed.

You dash down the street and zoom round the corner. Then, as fast as you can, you duck into a paper shop.

Maybe the ghost didn't notice where you went. You hope.

The owner glances up as you come in. "May I help you?" he asks.

"No," you say. "I'm just looking."

You head over to the magazine stand at the back of the shop. It's tall and you're hoping the ghost won't see you behind it. You spend about twenty minutes browsing through the comics.

When you think the coast is clear, you start to leave.

"Hold it right there," the owner says. He comes out from behind the counter and grabs your arm. "I'm calling the cops on you!"

Huh? Since when is reading comics against the law?

Find out on PAGE 119.

"I've found the head!" you call out when you reach the landing. You clutch the moose nervously. You peer into the darkness, trying to find the headless ghost.

The woman's body materializes on the steps below you.

"Good," her voice says. You still can't figure out how she can talk. "Just set it down right there—on the stairs."

Really? you think. This is going to work? Maybe the ghost hasn't seen the moose head, yet. What will she do when she discovers what you've done?

Trembling, you set the moose head down on the bottom step. You hold your breath.

For a moment, nothing happens.

Then the moose head begins to shake. At first it just rocks from side to side a little. But soon it starts to vibrate wildly.

The moose head begins to glow, as if there were a light inside it. Then a ghostly woman's face appears *inside* the moose head! You can't believe it! But there it is—the face of a beautiful young woman trapped within the dusty old moose head.

WOW! You did it! You actually found her head!

Turn to PAGE 51.

"Okay," you tell the ghost. "It's a deal."

"Good," the boy says with a strange smile.

"But you've got to really scare Lark," Robin warns, pointing a finger at the ghost.

"No problem," the ghost answers. "Wait here."

You and Robin stand on the front lawn in the moonlight. You watch the ghost as he floats into the house—right through the wall! A few minutes later, the screaming starts.

"Aaaaaah! Hellllpp! Aaaaaahhhhh! Noooooooo!" you hear Lark and his friends crying from inside. They sound as if they're face to face with sheer terror. Scared out of their minds.

Robin is really happy. But as the screaming continues, you start to worry. "You don't think he's really hurting them or anything, do you?" you ask.

"I don't know," Robin says. "Maybe we should go in there and stop him."

"Yeah," you say, swallowing hard.

The two of you start towards the front door. But just then the screams stop.

The ghost floats out through the front door.

"Okay," he says. "I've finished. See you tomorrow at ten."

Turn to PAGE 50.

You take the ghost-boy's hand.

As soon as you touch him, a chill runs through you. His hand feels like ice.

"Hold on," he says. "Here we go!"

Before you know what's happening, he starts to move away—floating sideways. His thin transparent body is floating right through the coffin—and he's taking you with him!

BOOM!

Inside your head, you hear the sound of fireworks. You close your eyes and *see* fireworks, too! At the same time, you feel your body being pulled through the coffin walls.

When the fireworks stop, you slowly open your eyes.

You instantly wish you hadn't.

You are lying on a dirt floor. Over your head is a dirt ceiling. The cave-like room is filled with an eerie green light. Stairways leading nowhere are covered in plush carpeting. Cobwebs drip from furniture. Laughs and moans echo all around you.

But the worst news is—you are surrounded by ghosts. That's right, you are in an underground world of living dead people. All of them floating around. Some dance, some play games, some wander aimlessly. But all of them are, well, dead.

Turn to PAGE 76.

The lights are out. All the lights. And you're scared to death. You can't move.

You stand there frozen in Robin's kitchen, in the dark.

"Come on," Robin says, grabbing your arm. "We'd better get out of here. Lark's coming!"

"No," you try to say. But you can't even speak. Your heart is pounding too hard. Your legs are locked stiff.

Robin tries to drag you out of the kitchen. But your hand grips the kitchen worktop.

"Oh, okay," Robin says. "We'll hide under the sink."

Quickly, he squats down and opens the two cabinet doors that lead to the space under the kitchen sink. He starts to crawl in.

Good idea, you think. Let's hide from the dark! Huh?

No. It doesn't make any sense. But you're so scared, you don't know *what* you're doing!

So you squat down and crawl into the cramped space with all the drainpipes and stuff.

That's when you see them. Two small eyes—glowing at you in the dark!

Turn to PAGE 128.

"Where are you going?" you ask the ghost-boy. "And what's your name?"

"You'll see," he answers.

"I'll see? I'll *see* what your name is?" you ask.

"Sure. It's on my gravestone," the ghost replies.

A cold mist swirls round the ghost-boy, making you shiver. You notice the ghost's eyes have turned hard. He's not so friendly, now.

You really regret making that promise.

"Let's go," he orders, leading the way.

You have no choice. You've seen this ghost in action. If you don't do what he says, he'll probably haunt and torment you for the rest of your life.

You follow him to an old graveyard. This one's on the far side of town. At the edge of the graveyard, the ghost stops. He puts out his hand to keep you from taking another step.

"Wait here, until I reach my tombstone," he tells you. "When you see me disappear, stand on top of my grave."

Hmmm. Sounds creepy. Are you going to do it?

If yes, turn to PAGE 90.
If no, turn to PAGE 110.

You decide to find out who is making all the noise in the attic.

You glance round for something to use as a weapon.

Let's see. Your grandmother has doilies. A rocking chair. Pillows. Not much to choose from. Finally you pick up a piece of rope that your mum used to tie your suitcase closed. You have no idea how a piece of rope could help, but it's all you've got.

The pounding of heavy feet over your head makes you wonder if you're making a mistake. But you have to find out who—or what!—is in the attic. Slowly, you climb the stairs. Dust from the attic steps stirs in the air and makes you sneeze.

"Ah-choo!" you say loudly.

All at once, the stomping stops.

The door to the attic bangs open.

"NO!" you scream when you see what's standing at the top of the stairs.

Go to PAGE 92.

MacFarling never told you what to do about an iron hand!

"Help!" you scream. "HELP!"

But who can help you in a graveyard?

You try to yank the metal hand off your arm. But you can't do it. Its grip is too strong.

"Help!" you cry again. But your scream dies in your throat. You are too terrified to make a sound. Because the hand is moving!

The iron fist creeps along your arm. It clutches your flesh so hard you can already feel the bruises. The glinting metal hand travels up to your throat. Horrified, you watch helplessly as the iron fingers open with a clanking sound and then snap around your neck. It's strangling you! You've got to do something fast!

Turn to PAGE 116.

No way. You're not going to practise your piano now.

"No, thanks," you tell Mrs Hatfield. "I never liked piano lessons. And now that I'm a ghost, I'm never going to practise again!"

Mrs Hatfield looks around at the other ghosts. They all smile and nod. Then she breaks into a huge grin.

"Good!" Mrs Hatfield says. "You passed the test!"

"What test?" you ask, feeling confused.

"You never were any good on that piano," she says. "In fact, you were simply terrible. I just wanted to be sure you didn't waste any more time with it. The world has enough bad musicians. It doesn't need another one."

Hmmph! you think. But you know she's right.

"Okay," Mrs Hatfield says, motioning to the ghost-boy. "You can take this one back."

Before you know what's happening, the ghost-boy pulls your hand again. This time, he drags you towards the mirror—and right into it. You close your eyes, and once again you hear fireworks. But halfway through the journey, he lets go of your hand. When you open your eyes, you are standing all alone in the cemetery. And you know you have finally come to

THE END.

You go into the house to look for John Luck-meyer. After all, you think he might be the Keeper of the Sword.

Are you *serious*?

Luckmeyer? You think *he* might hold the most powerful sword? The sword that can destroy the MPG? And didn't MacFarling warn you to stay away from that practical joker?

Uh-oh. If you think that, you may have a serious problem.

Take this test to find out:

THREE TRUE-OR-FALSE QUESTIONS TO DETERMINE IF SOMEONE IS CRAZY.

1.) Spinach is an alien life-form and should therefore never be eaten for dinner. TRUE or FALSE?

2.) The characters in your favourite TV programmes actually live in your television set. TRUE or FALSE?

3.) The marshmallow crop was ruined this year by a terrible freeze in Florida. TRUE or FALSE?

For your score, turn to PAGE 117.

So far everything seems normal. Just like all the other times you've spent the night at Robin's. In fact, you and Robin are having a great time. Even Robin's older brother Lark is less obnoxious than usual.

Yeah, Robin and Lark. Robin's last name is Birdsey. His parents like cute stuff like that.

Lark is having a sleep-over party. His friends are in eighth grade. They think they're really cool. And they are. Until nine o'clock. When suddenly all the lights in the house go out.

"Hey!" Lark yells at you and Robin. "Quit playing with the circuit-breakers, you little twerps. Or else!"

Uh-oh.

You didn't touch the circuit-breakers. Neither did Robin. And his parents aren't home.

Who's left?

That's right—the ghost.

And all the lights are out.

What now?

If you're afraid of the dark, turn to PAGE 83.
If you're okay in a pitch-black house, turn to PAGE 19.

You do as the ghost says. You wait at the edge of the graveyard until he stops at a grave. Then you watch as his whole airy body seems to disappear into the ground!

Okay, you think. This is it. Time to walk over there and stand on that grave.

You gulp loudly. You scratch your head. You burp.

Hey—enough stalling. Get over there!

Your legs tremble as you walk to the grave and peer at the headstone. Then, still shaking, you stand on the grave. The tombstone says JAMES T. REDDSON III. 1875–1910.

Hmmm. You do some quick maths and realize this bloke was thirty-five when he died. This can't be the kid's grave, you realize. He lied to you!

Before you can work out what you should do, you hear a terrible rumbling. You fling out your arms, trying desperately to keep your balance as the ground begins to shake. The earth all around you rises and rolls in waves. Your eyes open wide as you watch the ground beneath your feet break apart.

Get me out of here, you think. But you're too late.

A hand—the ghost-boy's hand!—suddenly pops up out of the dirt and grabs your ankle!

Go on to PAGE 115.

"Oh, no!" you gasp.

You stare at the map—and at the message spelled out on the gravestones.

YOU WILL DI SOON.

So that's the terrible message the graves are moving around to spell. And is the "you" you? Or is the curse directed at your grandma? Either way, it's super bad news!

"Mac," you say. "There's only one letter missing! Only one more coffin has to creep into place and then . . ."

"Then the curse will be complete," Mac says. He turns and walks back to his car.

"Wait!" you call after him.

He stops, but only long enough to pull out a business card. "Here," he says. "Call me after you defeat the Keeper of the Sword. Then I'll tell you what to do next."

Then he jumps back in his VW Beetle, leaving you standing in front of your grandmother's house. "Oh," he calls as he starts to drive off. "Two things to remember. Be sure to find out the name of the Keeper of the Sword. And stay away from the Luckmeyer twins!"

The Luckmeyer twins? you think.

If you've met the Luckmeyer twins already, turn to PAGE 8.

If you haven't met them, turn to PAGE 64.

You can't believe your eyes.

At the top of the attic stairs is a ghost horse! A huge, wild stallion, with its mane flying behind it. Foam drips from the stallion's mouth. Its eyes are wild with fury.

The horse backs up a step, then rears up and lets out a terrible angry cry. Its hooves crash down, clomping loudly on the attic floor.

Wait a minute, you think. Was there a horse buried in the cemetery?

Then you remember. An extra-large grave with a headstone that read:

HERE LIES GLORY. TOO WILD FOR THE RIDERS OF THIS WORLD.

No kidding, you think. This horse looks like a killer!

Quick. You're going to be trampled—unless you do something.

But what?

If you jump on Glory and ride him, turn to PAGE 126.

If you use the rope to lasso him, turn to PAGE 54.

You turn on your heels and run as fast as you can—straight towards the graveyard!

"Hey!" Jane calls to you. "Don't go in there!"

Oh, sure, you think. She just doesn't want you to escape! You keep running.

But the minute you cross the property line—from your grandmother's garden into the cemetery—a terrible chill runs down your spine.

Your whole body feels as if it has turned to ice. Or stone. You stop running and begin to move very slowly.

"I am walking among the dead," you hear yourself say in a flat voice. Why did I say that? you wonder.

"You are walking among the dead," John says right behind you. He and Jane float around the graveyard.

"I am a prisoner of the graves," you hear yourself say.

"You are a prisoner of the graves." John and Jane repeat your words together.

You take a few more steps. Your legs are so stiff, you can barely move.

You look down at your feet—and scream.

"Aaahhh!" you moan. "My feet have turned to stone!"

Go on to PAGE 77.

Okay. So you're not a natural-born cowboy.

You're just a kid with a dumb rope in your hands—and a foaming-at-the-mouth horse about to trample you on the stairs.

You wave the rope at the horse, using it like a wimpy whip. You feel so stupid, you're surprised the horse doesn't start laughing.

But someone does laugh! You turn round and see a ghostly cowboy floating your way.

"Worst attempt I've ever seen," the cowboy says. You stare at him with your mouth open. He takes the rope from you.

"You want to lasso Glory, you're gonna need some lessons from a expert. Me!" The cowboy gives the rope a sharp yank and, *FLICK*, it lands round the stallion's neck.

"Cool!" you cheer. "Can you show me how to do that?"

"Sure thing, pardner," the cowboy answers. "Now here's what you have to do."

For the next hour the ghost-cowboy teaches you all about lassoing.

When you think you're ready, try to lasso Glory all by yourself on PAGE 58.

"Robin," you whisper, "I hate to tell you this, but we're hiding under the sink with a Lanx."

"A what?" Robin asks.

"A Lanx! A Lanx!" You are practically shouting. "It's like a Grool, but worse!"

Robin stares at you. Then he shakes his head. "You are getting too weird. Even for me."

"It looks like a potato," you continue, "but it has really sharp teeth!" You have to make Robin believe you! You are in terrible danger.

"That's it," Robin says. He pops open the cabinet door. "Fun's over. You know," he adds as he crawls out from under the sink, "I didn't really believe your ghost story, either. I was just playing along."

You gaze sadly at Robin as he heads out of the kitchen. You have a feeling you've just lost your best friend.

"Heh heh heh," you hear behind you.

You glance back at the glowing eyes. They look even brighter than before.

You thought being followed home by a ghost was a problem. Wait until you try living with a Lanx!

"Heh heh heh."

THE END

96

You race out to the graveyard. You've got to find the fencing woman's grave—fast! Then it hits you. You only know her first name. Sarah.

Sarah who?

You run up and down the rows of tombstones, searching for a grave marked Sarah. Naturally, you find two.

One is Sarah Grayson. Born in 1820. Died in 1895.

The other is Sarah McGinnis. Born 1918. Died 1940.

It's up to you. Which is the right Sarah?

Think very carefully.

Then pick one.

You balance the sword under one arm and feel around in your pockets. You pull a broken pencil from your jeans. You glance down and find a crumpled gum wrapper on the ground. You grab it and with shaking fingers you write down the year of Sarah's death.

And hope you've chosen correctly!

Have you written down the date of Sarah's death? Good. Because something terrifying is happening behind you. You really don't want to keep your back turned. So put down your pencil and turn to PAGE 114. If you dare . . .

"Get away from me!" you shout. You duck and twist, trying to avoid the diving chickens. They squawk and flap their wings. One bird lands on your shoulder. Its claws dig into your clothes.

"Hey!" you yell at it. You try shaking it off, but it clings to you. You notice the other chickens hovering near by.

You reach up to grab the stupid bird but something stops you. Could it be? Is the chicken *smiling* at you?

You peer closely at the bird.

Uh-oh.

That chicken isn't smiling, it's baring its teeth.

But chickens don't have teeth. And they definitely don't have fangs.

That's right. Fangs. Guess what? These aren't ordinary chickens. These are vampire chickens. And the bird on your shoulder is leaning closer. And closer. And closer.

CHOMP!

Being bitten by a vampire chicken puts you in a fowl mood. Oh, well. Better cluck next time.

THE END

"No," you tell the ghost. "I've kept my promise. And look where it got me!"

"Suit yourself," the ghost-boy says. He vanishes.

So, now what are you going to do, huh? Just lie there in the coffin and rot?

That's one choice.

Got any other ideas?

Okay, sure. You could start screaming at the top of your lungs. Maybe—just maybe—someone will hear you.

Like who?

Like the cemetery caretaker. He shows up once a week. On Fridays.

Well? What day is this?

If you are reading this on Friday, turn to PAGE 13.

If you are not reading this on Friday, turn to PAGE 107.

You decide to duel with the woman in the fencing costume. She's not as big as the soldier.

"*En garde*, yourself!" you cry. You notice that as soon as you shouted at the woman, the soldier-ghost vanished.

The fencer glides towards you, approaching slowly. You feel around desperately for something you can use as a weapon. The whole time you keep your eyes glued to the sharp tip of her sword. Or rather, her *foil*. That's what a fencing sword is called.

The fencer keeps coming towards you, slowly . . . slowly. Beads of sweat break out along your upper lip. The tip of the foil wavers slightly, as if the fencer were deciding on the perfect spot to stab you.

Finally your fingers grasp something leaning against the wall. An umbrella. It's not much. But it'll have to do.

You grab it and strike a fencing pose.

"*En garde!*" you shout again.

The fencer freezes, her foil raised.

Then in a flash, she lunges at you!

Quick! Find out if you're still alive on PAGE 122.

100

You jump back, trying to make room for Robin. He's backing up faster than a pizza delivery man who's missed the address.

But the knife keeps coming anyway.

Quick—you have to do something to help him!

You spot a baseball bat in the corner of the room.

Hmm. Good choice. If you have a good aim.

But there's also a huge needle-point pillow on Robin's bed. One that his mother made for him. Maybe you should use it as a shield.

Choose your weapon.

If you use the baseball bat, turn to PAGE 35.
If you use the pillow as a shield, turn to PAGE 46.

"Ow!" Robin cries out. His hand flies up to his cheek, where the juggling ball hit him.

Your mouth falls open. This is terrible. The ghost must have followed you down the street!

"Why did you do that?" Robin yells. "That really hurt!"

"But I didn't do it!" you reply. "It was that ghost!"

Robin stares at the juggling balls. They're just lying on the floor now. The ghost is nowhere in sight.

"Yeah, right," Robin says. "Like I'm really going to believe in ghosts. Come on, how did you do that?"

Before you can answer, there's a knock on Robin's bedroom door. He walks over and opens it.

"Yikes!" he screams.

Floating in the doorway, in mid-air, is a long sharp carving knife.

And it's pointed right at Robin's heart!

Robin is backing away fast, so you'd better move back, too. Back to PAGE 100.

102

Using the back door you quietly slip into the house. Then you sneak up the back staircase to the first floor. You peek round the corner carefully—you don't want to run into the Luckmeyers. When you are sure the coast is clear, you start up the stairs towards the attic.

As soon as you step into the stairway, you see a huge soldier standing at the top of the second-floor landing!

His uniform is old-fashioned. Civil War, you guess. And judging from the medals pinned to his grey jacket, this man knows what he's doing.

And what he's doing right now is pulling a sword from its holder.

The sword is about a metre and a half long. The handle is mother-of-pearl, encrusted with sapphires. The blade gleams. Even in the darkness you can see that it's dangerously sharp.

The enormous soldier points the sword at your heart. "Do not advance one more step—unless you are willing to die!" he booms.

Go on to PAGE 104.

"Get him, Sparkle!" you shout.

The hideous ghost floats towards you. The worms wriggle through his matted hair. This ghost is disgusting!

"Woof!" Sparkle barks right in the ghost's disgusting face.

Nothing happens.

"Uh, again, Sparkle!" you command. But Sparkle tucks his tail between his legs, whimpers and slinks away.

"Sparkle, come back," you call. But it's no use. That's one terrified mutt. You turn to face the wormy ghost.

The ghost brings his face right next to yours. The worms wiggle from the ghost to you. They crawl in your mouth, up your nose, in your ears.

Is it possible to die from being completely nauseated?

Well, even if it isn't, the worms make it impossible for you to breathe. Making this

THE END.

104

You can't take your eyes off the sword. The longer you stare at it, the more your legs shake.

Then it dawns on you. This soldier must be the Keeper of the Sword!

So what are you going to do? Run and hide? Definitely!

Trembling in fear, you start to back away. That's when you feel a sharp point sticking you in the back. Right between your shoulder blades.

"Ouch!" you cry out, turning round.

Big trouble. Behind you is *another* ghost. And this one's dressed in a fencing costume. White canvas trousers. A wire mesh mask. Leather gloves.

"*En garde!*" the new ghost says. The voice echoes all around you. From the voice, you know this ghost is a woman.

Then you realize something. She has a sword, too!

Two ghosts. Two swords. Both dangerous. But only one has the sword you need.

Which one?

If you think the fencer is the Keeper of the Sword, turn to PAGE 99.

If you think it's the soldier, turn to PAGE 118.

The book landed with the front cover face up. That means you don't survive the fall from the bridge.

Sorry.

So now you are a ghost, roaming the neighbourhood, haunting everyone in sight. And for a while, scaring people is fun.

But soon you get tired of people screaming whenever you appear. And some people can't even see you. For some reason, not everyone is able to see ghosts.

You begin to understand why the Luckmeyer twins played pranks and practical jokes. It's a laugh!

So you start doing it, too—playing tricks on people. You move their coffee cups while they're not looking. You raise their windows right after they've closed them. You wrinkle their clothes while they're ironing them. You steal key pieces from jigsaw puzzles when people aren't looking.

Then one day, you go too far—you do something really evil. You go through a GIVE YOUR-SELF GOOSEBUMPS book with a black felt marker and cross off all the page numbers!

The only problem is, it was *this* book. The only one you're in.

Which is why, sad to say, this is really and truly . . .

THE END.

106

"Wha-what do you mean, *all* of you?" you manage to stammer.

"You ask too many questions!" Uh-oh. Elvira's eyes flash green again. "Don't get in our way and *maybe* we will let you live."

She soars up over your head and glares down at you. "And don't you go talking to that ghost-hunter MacFarling, either!" Elvira adds.

In the next instant, she floats backwards and disappears into the wall.

MacFarling? A ghost-hunter?

You are startled by loud clumping footsteps above you. You glance up at the ceiling. The light fixture is shaking. It sounds as if a whole crowd wearing clunky boots is stomping around in the attic.

Who could it be?

If you want to find out about MacFarling, turn to PAGE 16.

If you want to find out who's in the attic, turn to PAGE 85.

Okay, time to face facts. Today is not Friday. The caretaker is not going to show up for a long time.

And guess what else? If he did show up, he probably wouldn't hear you screaming anyway. After all, you're two metres underground.

Looks like you're running out of choices. Maybe you'd better go and take the cold, cold hand of that ghost-boy after all.

Turn to PAGE 82.

108

You run up the steps, darting sideways to get past John.

But he grabs you with one hand. Whoa! For a see-through boy, John is strong! In his other hand he dangles a ghostly snake before your eyes.

YIKES! The snake hisses in your face. Its fangs drip ghostly poison.

John and Jane laugh at your terrified expression. John shoves the hissing snake into your face again. Its tongue darts in and out between its razor-sharp fangs.

Can a ghost snake hurt you? The pain where John is clutching your arm makes you think it probably can!

You swallow hard and lurch away from him. Luckily, he and Jane don't try to follow.

With a yank, you pull open your grandmother's kitchen door.

YIKES, AGAIN! That other ghost—Elvira—is standing right there!

"So you came back," she snarls. "You may regret that!"

She turns and floats into the hall. Then she floats up the stairs.

Towards *your* room.

Follow her to PAGE 49.

Robin picks up a worm from the plate. He stares at it. Just as he opens his mouth to take a bite, you hear someone sniggering.

You glance round.

The bushes seem to be moving.

Quickly, you inch over towards the sound.

"He's eating it!" you hear a voice whisper. A voice that sounds exactly like Robin's brother, Lark. "Ha, ha. The little twerp! I hope he chokes!"

"Yeah," another voice says. "That was a cool deal we made with the ghost. Pretending to scream for an hour. And then he promised to make your brother eat worms the next day."

Oh, no! you realize. You've been tricked!

Go on to PAGE 130.

You decide not to follow the ghost into the cemetery.

Why should I? you think. Just because I promised him I would?

You feel a little guilty about breaking your promise.

But as soon as the ghost disappears into the grave, you turn and run as fast as you can. All the way back home.

And you know what happens next?

Nothing.

That's right. Nothing. And you never see another ghost again, as long as you live.

Years later, you tell your children all about your grandmother's haunted house. About how a ghost followed you home. And haunted your best friend's brother's party. And you promised to follow him into the graveyard the next day, but didn't do it.

Your children think you're making it up, of course. But you know the truth.

Because every time you walk past a graveyard, you hear voices calling you. Accusing you. The voices of the ghost-boy and all his ghost friends. "Yooooooou," they call. "Yooooou lied!"

THE END

You press the button to change the channel again.

Unfortunately, you've run out of channels. Even with Direct TV, a satellite dish, and all the cable channels in the universe combined, you can only go so far. Then you hit the end of the line.

257,000 channels—and nothing on.

So when you press the button for a higher channel, nothing happens. The Neanderthal man doesn't change into anything else.

And you know what that means. It means you've just been hit on the head with a big ugly club!

Ow. That hurt. And he's taking aim again!

Oh, well. That's what you get for trying to survive this ugly episode by *pushing buttons*!

Seriously—didn't it ever occur to you to just *duck*?

THE END

112

You decide to tell your grandmother the truth.

Wait a minute. Are you kidding?

You're going to tell your grandmother that her house is haunted? That the big mess in the kitchen was a ghoulish prank? That there are so many ghosts around that Mac MacFarling, professional ghost-hunter, wouldn't take the case?

You're going to tell her all that?

Oh, REALLY?

Well just try it. Go and tell your parents—or your grandparents—the same story. See if they believe you.

HA!

When they've finished laughing, you can start reading again on PAGE 71.

And try to learn a little lesson from this: you should always try to tell the truth. But sometimes the truth is too unbelievable to tell. Like any time ghosts are involved.

That's when you have to be a little creative . . .

Turn to PAGE 71.

So there you are, standing like a stone statue in a graveyard. You probably think this is the end, don't you?

Well, it *could* have been.

But a few days later, the graveyard caretaker comes by. He notices you—and realizes that you don't belong there. Pretty soon, he figures out he could get a lot of money for a stone statue of a kid!

So he backs his pick-up truck into the cemetery and loads you on it. Then he drives away. He sells you to a garden shop that sells stone statues to put in people's gardens.

A few months later, your grandmother walks into the shop and sees you standing there. She can't believe her eyes—a statue that looks exactly like her missing grandchild! She buys you and brings you back to her house.

Unfortunately, your grandmother's house is still haunted. But for some reason, she has never noticed the ghosts floating all around.

But you notice them. Especially the two ghosts you hate the most—the Luckmeyer twins! They spend the rest of eternity teasing you and pinching your stone nose. And you just have to stand there and take it until

THE END OF TIME.

114

You don't like the prickly feeling on the back of your neck. You turn round slowly—and gasp.

The coffins have moved again!

You can tell because you've wandered to the front of the graveyard. You are standing by the first row. The row that spelled out YOU in the curse. The row that used to have only three tombstones.

But now the front row is crowded with graves. Seven of them. Four more coffins have crept into place!

You glance towards the back of the graveyard and notice new empty spots. It's true! The tombstones are spelling again!

Your heart pounds as you run along the row, reading the four new names—trying to see what the new initials will spell out.

Bannister. Oswald. Thackery. Hamilton.

B . . . O . . . T . . . H.

Oh, no!

Now the message reads YOU *BOTH* WILL DI SOON!

Quick! Hurry to PAGE 31.

The ghost-boy grips your ankle so hard, you think he might break your bones.

You try to yank your leg away, but it's no use. The ghost-boy won't let go. And he's strong. Super strong.

Oh, no! you realize. He's not just holding on to your ankle. He's pulling you right into the ground with him!

He's pulling you down into the grave beneath your feet!

Hang on until you get to PAGE 17.

116

The metal hand clutching your throat is squeezing the life out of you. You don't have much time left.

Then you see it. The sword. It has lifted itself out of the ground—and it's once again floating in mid-air. The sword helped before. Maybe it can help you again.

Stretching your arm as far as you can, you reach for the sword. You nearly topple over, but you manage to grab the handle. Now that you have the sword, you're not sure what to do with it. But you have to do something—the fingers are tightening . . . tightening . . .

You've got to get some space between your throat and the metal fingers! You bring the sword up to your neck. Trying to avoid slicing your own throat, you jostle and jiggle the sword through the fingers of the metal hand. Finally, the blade pokes up through the iron fist. The tip is just under your nose. The sword is jammed between your skin and the cold metal of Brandon Estep's hand.

The iron hand releases your throat. The sword and the hand clatter to the ground. It's over.

Well, maybe not.

The moment the sword hits the dirt, you hear a sound. An almost deafening sound.

Hold your ears and turn to PAGE 131.

If you answered TRUE to any of the questions in the test, you should not continue reading this book.

Close it—and wait for the men in the white coats to come and take you away. Don't worry. You'll be fine after a nice long rest . . .

On the other hand, if you answered FALSE to all the test questions, there may be hope for you.

But you've got to face facts. John Luckmeyer is not the Keeper of the Sword. The Keeper of the Sword is a much scarier, much more terrifying ghost.

Turn to PAGE 8, face reality and choose again.

118

You decide the enormous Civil War soldier must be the Keeper of the Sword. You face him and the fencing-ghost behind you vanishes.

You can't seem to lift your eyes from the sharp blade of the soldier's weapon. "Are y-y-you the K-Keeper of the Sword?" you ask him, your voice trembling.

"NO!" he bellows.

Then he lunges forward and charges at you!

"Aaaaahhh!" you scream in terror. You turn and run for your life. Down the stairs. Out of the front door. Into the night.

You don't look back. But you don't have to. You can hear the ghostly soldier behind you. His heavy boots thud against the ground.

You dash across the front garden, towards the road. You manage to put some distance between you and the ghost. But then something grabs your foot!

SMACK. Your hands hit the gravel at the side of the road as you fall flat on your face. You glance down to see what made you fall. Just a gnarled tree root.

"Prepare to die!" the soldier shouts as he stomps towards you.

Quick! Rush to PAGE 24.

"What did I do?" you ask the shop owner.

"You know perfectly well," the owner says. "Shoplifting!"

Then he reaches round behind your back—and pulls out a comic book!

"Huh?" you say. "Where did that come from?"

"Don't try to kid me," the owner says. "I could see it plain as day." He smacks you on the forehead with the rolled-up comic book. "Did you really think you'd get away with tucking this into the waistband of your jeans? It wasn't even under your shirt! I don't know how you balanced it that way. It was hardly tucked into your jeans at all."

You are dumbfounded. Speechless. You didn't steal that comic book! Honest!

But then you hear the ghost sniggering in your ear.

"Welcome to your new career," the ghost says.

To make a long story short, the ghost follows you the rest of your life—getting you into trouble every step of the way. He takes money from your mother's purse—and plants it in your dresser. He steals cars—and parks them in *your* driveway. Everywhere you go, things disappear. And people blame you.

In fact, you probably didn't pay for this book, did you? Well, just for that, you're facing . . .

THE END.

"I suppose Brandon's ghost is finally at rest," you say.

You gaze around you and see that the tombstones are all back where they belong. In fact, the whole graveyard looks quite sleepy and peaceful.

"Oh, don't be a goose," your grandmother scolds. "There are no ghosts. Next, you'll be telling me that the ghost of Elmyra Martin is taking a nap in your room!"

Elvira? You'd forgotten about her. But you suppose when the other ghosts returned to their graves, Elvira did, too.

Your grandmother yawns. "Come on," she says sleepily. "This is way past both our bedtimes."

You and your grandmother go inside. You say good-night and climb the stairs to your bedroom.

What a day! you think, flopping down on the soft bed.

"Watch it!" a familiar voice echoes through the room. A lump under the duvet slowly materializes.

Elvira!

"Don't hog the covers," she snaps. She yanks the blanket under you so hard you roll right out of bed.

You've heard of bad room-mates, but this is ridiculous. Well, you'll just have to learn to get along. Because Elvira is here for eternity. Your days of having your own room have come to an

END.

You and Robin watch as the ghost forms himself into a funnel-shaped tornado again.

"Uh-oh," Robin whispers to you. "If he does what I think he's going to do, I wouldn't want to be Lark. It hurts!"

In the next instant, the ghost blows himself into Lark's head. He flows into one ear—and out the other.

"Yeow!" Lark screams. "Okay okay okay okay okay! I'll do it!"

Robin turns to you and slaps you five. "Cool!" he says.

"Not so fast," the ghost says. "You've still got some eating to do."

"We have?" you say.

"A deal's a deal," the ghost says.

Right.

Ah, well. Maybe eating worms won't be so bad in

THE END.

122

The tip of the blade slices right through your neck!

Okay, you can open your eyes now. Good news. You're still alive. And you never felt a thing. You know why?

The fencer is a ghost. She's not solid. She's airy. See-through. And so is her weapon.

You pick up your umbrella and slice back. You lunge forwards, poking your umbrella right between her ribs.

But your umbrella has the same effect on *her* that her foil has on you! None.

There's no point in keeping up this duel. Neither of you can win. You put down the umbrella.

"Are you the Keeper of the Sword?" you ask her.

"Yes," she says. She reaches up and pulls off her mask.

You gasp and your stomach turns over.

She doesn't have a face. Because she doesn't have a *head*!

"Yes. This is the sword you need," she tells you. You wonder where her voice is coming from. "And I will give it to you—if you can find my head."

Is she kidding? What are the chances?

Maybe you should just try to grab the sword.

If you grab the sword, turn to PAGE 21.
If you look for her head, turn to PAGE 62.

"I know what you're thinking," Mrs Hatfield says. "You're afraid you can't get to the gold, now that you're here, with us."

You nod.

"But don't worry," she says. "You didn't come here the . . . the normal way. So you can go back to the world of the living any time you want."

Your eyes light up. "I can?" you say. "How?"

"Oh, it's easy," Mrs Hatfield says. "Haven't you ever seen *The Wizard of Oz*?"

Huh?

"*You* know," she goes on. "All you have to do is click your heels together three times and say, 'There's no place like home.' It worked in the film. It should work here, too."

Is she kidding? Well, what have you got to lose?

So, you give it a try. You click your trainers together three times and say, "There's no place like home." When you open your eyes again, you're in your own bed at home.

With the map in your hand!

Hey. Your mum always said those piano lessons would pay off someday, didn't she? Looks like she was right!

THE END

You hurry into the hall and start up the stairs towards your room. But something stops you.

A terrible chill in the air. A cold so cold, you feel as if it will freeze your blood and bones.

An instant later, thirteen howling ghosts appear. They float out of the walls and come towards you. They are all shapes and sizes, but they have one thing in common.

They are all terrifying!

NO! you want to cry. This can't be happening!

Your knees shake so much, you almost fall down. But somehow you manage to run. Ghostly arms reach for you as you race out of the front door. Into the front garden, where the sky is growing dark.

For the next ten minutes, you huddle under a big tree, trying to think.

Mostly, you just think one thing. GET ME OUT OF HERE!

But you know you can't go home. Your parents are away on holiday. Besides, you can't leave your grandmother here all alone. Not with those creeping coffins.

Which means you've got to go back into that house. You've got to get rid of the ghosts. And you've got to find the Keeper of the Sword. Before it's too late!

Go on to PAGE 102.

You decide to sit down and wait. If the MPG is so powerful, you think, then let him come to me!

With the fencing foil in your hand, you plop down on a chair in the hall. Sparkle, your grandma's mutt, comes and sits at your feet. You feel better knowing someone's on your side—even if it is just an old dog.

A loud knocking begins inside the walls. A moment later, a ghost floats through the wall towards you. A creepy ghost without eyes!

"Ooooo," he moans sadly. He hovers closer.

You stand up and hold out the foil. Your hands tremble. Is this the MPG?

Sparkle jumps to his feet, too. "Arrf! Arrf-arf!" the dog barks.

The ghost instantly disappears!

Did Sparkle do that? "Hey, Sparkle," you say, patting the dog's head. "Good job!"

A minute later, you hear a terrible groaning sound. Another ghost appears in the hall. This one has worms crawling all over his face!

A low growl begins in Sparkle's throat.

Will it work again? Will Sparkle scare away the ghost?

Find out on PAGE 103.

As the ghost-horse charges at you, you grab his mane and pull yourself on to his back.

Yee-haw! Ride 'em, cowboy!

There's only one problem. An instant later, the horse turns left.

And a left turn from your grandmother's attic stairway goes only one place. Straight *through* the stairway wall.

And then outside!

Uh-oh.

You grip Glory's mane even tighter and shut your eyes.

Okay, you think. Makes sense. A ghost-horse can ride through walls.

But can you?

BAM.

Guess not.

And that's why, when you open your eyes again, you're still riding Glory! You and your ghost-horse charge through the moonlit sky. As you will—for eternity.

It said on his tombstone, Glory was "too wild for the riders of this world". But face it, you aren't of *this* world any more. Those days have come to an

END.

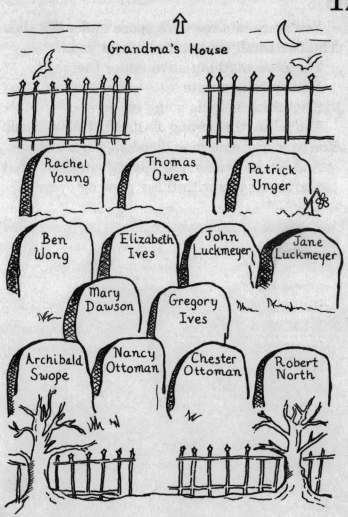

The Rest of the Graveyard

Turn to PAGE 65.

You stare into the dark space under the sink. The two small eyes stare back at you.

There's something alive under there!

Hey, wait a minute.

Something fishy is going on here.

You're in the wrong GOOSEBUMPS book! You're in *It Came from Beneath the Sink!*

And you have a terrible feeling you know what is staring at you with those glowing eyes.

If you think the eyes belong to a Grool, turn to PAGE 132.

If you think the eyes belong to a Lanx, turn to PAGE 95.

This time, the remote control changes the Egyptian pharaoh king into a Neanderthal man. You recognize him from all the science books at school. Big hairy bloke. Slumpy shoulders. Long arms. Huge wooden club.

Huge wooden club?

Yes.

And he's swinging it at your head!

Think fast!

If you change the channel again, turn to PAGE 111.

If you try the mute button, turn to PAGE 78.

"Stop!" you cry out, running over to Robin. "Don't eat the worms! It's a double-cross!"

"What?" Robin asks, looking confused. Luckily he was too disgusted to take a first bite.

You explain what you've overheard. "Your brother's in there!" you say, pointing to the bushes. "He's tricked us! He made a deal with the ghost. He pretended to scream last night— even though the ghost wasn't doing *anything* to him!"

Robin still looks confused. Until Lark and his friends come out laughing. "Ha, ha," they say. "You have to eat worms because of us. You twerps got what you deserved."

"What are *you* laughing about?" the ghost says to Lark. "You made a deal, too. I agreed to make your brother eat worms. But in return, you promised to do whatever I asked."

"Yeah," Lark says. "So what?"

"So now it's time to keep *your* part of the bargain," the ghost says to Lark. "And here it is: you have to spend the night with a dead rat— in an open grave!"

"Oh, right," Lark says. "And just how are you going to make me do that?"

"Easy," the ghost says with a small laugh.

Turn to PAGE 121.

BONG! BONG! BONG!

What *is* that? Some kind of clock tower?

BONG ... BONG ... BONG ... BONG ...

The chimes strike twelve times.

At exactly midnight, the iron hand and the sword vanish—and your grandmother appears in the doorway of her house.

"Why, listen to that!" she exclaims. "It's the clock tower in the church. That clock hasn't chimed in years!"

"Really?" you say, your eyes growing wide.

Your grandmother nods. "Not since Brandon Estep died. He crashed his motorcycle in this graveyard. Wild boy. But he loved that clock tower. He had helped his father build it. So everyone said Brandon haunted this place, and that's why the clock wouldn't chime. Of course that's a lot of nonsense."

Nonsense? No way, you think.

"They've tried to fix the clock a million times," your grandmother goes on. "But it's never worked. I wonder why it's started chiming now?"

You're pretty sure you know the answer to that.

Go to PAGE 120.

132

"Aaaaah," you shriek. "It's a Grool!"

"What are you talking about?" Robin whispers.

"Th-th-those eyes," you stammer. "They belong to an evil Grool!"

You are in big trouble now. The Grool loves to make terrible things happen. As if your luck wasn't *already* bad.

"You're crazy," Robin tells you. "And if you don't shut up, Lark and his buddies are going to find us."

"You thought I was crazy when I told you about the ghost," you hiss at Robin. "And now look at us."

Robin sees your point. "Okay." He sighs. "Let's check out this Grool."

You move aside so that Robin can see the glowing eyes for himself. He reaches for the Grool.

"Don't touch it!" you warn him. But it's too late. You can't watch. You shut your eyes.

"So this is a Grool!" Robin laughs. He holds something in front of your face. You open one eye. Then you open the other eye.

Robin is holding a little kitten.

"Oooops," you say sheepishly. "Sorry. I suppose I'm a little stressed. That happens to me when I meet ghosts."

Get back into the story on PAGE 67.

Reader beware – here's THREE TIMES the scare!

Look out for these bumper GOOSEBUMPS editions. With three spine-tingling stories by R.L. Stine in each book, get ready for three times the thrill ... three times the scare ... three times the GOOSEBUMPS!

COLLECTION 1
Welcome to Dead House
Say Cheese and Die
Stay Out of the Basement

COLLECTION 2
The Curse of the Mummy's Tomb
Let's Get Invisible!
Night of the Living Dummy

COLLECTION 3
The Girl Who Cried Monster
Welcome to Camp Nightmare
The Ghost Next Door

COLLECTION 4
The Haunted Mask
Piano Lessons Can Be Murder
Be Careful What You Wish For

COLLECTION 5
The Werewolf of Fever Swamp
You Can't Scare Me!
One Day at HorrorLand

COLLECTION 6
Why I'm Afraid of Bees
Deep Trouble
Go Eat Worms

COLLECTION 7
Return of the Mummy
The Scarecrow Walks at Midnight
Attack of the Mutant

COLLECTION 8
My Hairiest Adventure
A Night in Terror Tower
The Cuckoo Clock of Doom

COLLECTION 9
Ghost Beach
Phantom of the Auditorium
It Came From Beneath the Sink!

Goosebumps

R.L. Stine

Reader beware, you're in for a scare!

These terrifying tales will send shivers up your spine:

1	Welcome to Dead House
2	Say Cheese and Die!
3	Stay Out of the Basement
4	The Curse of the Mummy's Tomb
5	Monster Blood
6	Let's Get Invisible!
7	Night of the Living Dummy
8	The Girl Who Cried Monster
9	Welcome to Camp Nightmare
10	The Ghost Next Door
11	The Haunted Mask
12	Piano Lessons Can Be Murder
13	Be Careful What You Wish For
14	The Werewolf of Fever Swamp
15	You Can't Scare Me!
16	One Day at HorrorLand
17	Why I'm Afraid of Bees
18	Monster Blood II
19	Deep Trouble
20	Go Eat Worms
21	Return of the Mummy
22	The Scarecrow Walks at Midnight
23	Attack of the Mutant
24	My Hairiest Adventure
25	A Night in Terror Tower
26	The Cuckoo Clock of Doom
27	Monster Blood III
28	Ghost Beach
29	Phantom of the Auditorium

30	It Came From Beneath the Sink!
31	Night of the Living Dummy II
32	The Barking Ghost
33	The Horror at Camp Jellyjam
34	Revenge of the Garden Gnomes
35	A Shocker on Shock Street
36	The Haunted Mask II
37	The Headless Ghost
38	The Abominable Snowman of Pasadena
39	How I Got My Shrunken Head
40	Night of the Living Dummy III
41	Bad Hare Day
42	Egg Monsters From Mars
43	The Beast From the East
44	Say Cheese and Die – Again!
45	Ghost Camp
46	How to Kill a Monster
47	Legend of the Lost Legend
48	Attack of the Jack-O'-Lanterns
49	Vampire Breath
50	Calling All Creeps!
51	Beware, the Snowman
52	How I Learned to Fly
53	Chicken Chicken
54	Don't Go To Sleep!
55	The Blob That Ate Everyone
56	The Curse of Camp Cold Lake
57	My Best Friend is Invisible
58	Deep Trouble II
	The Haunted School
	Werewolf Skin
	I Live in Your Basement
	Monster Blood IV

Reader beware – you choose the scare!

Give Yourself Goosebumps

A scary new series from R.L. Stine – where *you* decide what happens!

1 Escape From the Carnival of Horrors
2 Tick Tock, You're Dead!
3 Trapped in Bat Wing Hall
4 The Deadly Experiments of Dr Eeek
5 Night in Werewolf Woods
6 Beware of the Purple Peanut Butter
7 Under the Magician's Spell
8 The Curse of the Creeping Coffin

Choose from over 20 scary endings!

HIPPO GHOST

**Secrets from the past... Danger in the present...
Hippo Ghost brings you the spookiest of tales...**

Castle of Ghosts
Carol Barton
Abbie's *bound* to see some ghosts at the castle where
her aunt works – isn't she?

The Face on the Wall
Carol Barton
Jeremy knows he must solve the mystery of the face on
the wall – however much it frightens him...

Summer Visitors
Carol Barton
Emma thinks she's in for a really boring summer, until she
meets the Carstairs family on the beach. But there's
something very *strange* about her new friends...

Ghostly Music
Richard Brown
Beth loves her piano lessons. So why have they started to
make her *ill*...?

A Patchwork of Ghosts
Angela Bull
Who is the evil-looking ghost tormenting Lizzie, and why
does he want to hurt her...?

The Ghosts who Waited
Dennis Hamley
Everything's changed since Rosy and her family moved
house. Why has everyone suddenly turned against her...?

The Railway Phantoms
Dennis Hamley
Rachel has visions. She dreams of two children in strange,
disintegrating clothes. And it seems as if they are trying
to contact her...

The Haunting of Gull Cottage
Tessa Krailing
Unless Kezzie and James can find what really happened in
Gull Cottage that terrible night many years ago, the
haunting may never stop...

The Hidden Tomb
Jenny Oldfield
Can Kate unlock the mystery of the curse on Middleton
Hall, before it destroys the Mason family...?

The House at the End of Ferry Road
Martin Oliver
The house at the end of Ferry Road has just been built.
So it can't be haunted, can it...?

Beware! This House is Haunted
This House is Haunted Too!
Lance Salway
Jessica doesn't believe in ghosts. So who *is* writing the
strange, spooky messages?

The Children Next Door
Jean Ure
Laura longs to make friends with the children next door.
But they're not quite what they seem...

The Girl in the Blue Tunic
Jean Ure
Who is the strange girl Hannah meets at school – and
why does she seem so alone?

HIPPO ANIMAL

Have you ever longed for a puppy to love, or a horse of your own? Have you ever wondered what it would be like to make friends with a wild animal? If so, then you're sure to fall in love with these fantastic titles from Hippo Animal!

Owl Cry
Deborah van der Beek
Can Solomon really look after an abandoned baby owl?

Thunderfoot
Deborah van der Beek
When Mel finds the enormous, neglected horse Thunderfoot, she doesn't know it will change her life for ever...

Vanilla Fudge
Deborah van der Beek
When Lizzie and Hannah fall in love with the same dog, neither of them will give up without a fight...

A Foxcub Named Freedom
Brenda Jobling
An injured vixen nudges her young son away from her. She can sense danger and cares nothing for herself – only for her son's freedom...

Goose on the Run

Brenda Jobling

It's an unusual pet – an injured Canada goose.
But soon Josh can't imagine being without him.
And the goose won't let *anyone* take him away
from Josh...

Pirate the Seal

Brenda Jobling

Ryan's always been lonely – but then he meets
Pirate and at last he has a real friend...

Animal Rescue

Bette Paul

Can Tessa help save the badgers of Delves Wood
from destruction?

Take Six Kittens

Bette Paul

James and Jenny's dad promises them a pet when
they move to the country. But they end up with
more than they bargained for...

Take Six Puppies

Bette Paul

Anna knows she shouldn't get attached to the
six new puppies at the Millington Farm Dog
Sanctuary, but surely it can't hurt to get just a
little bit fond of them...